Stars
at
Bedtime

DK
A Dorling Kindersley Book

LONDON, NEW YORK, MUNICH,
MELBOURNE, and DELHI

For Archie, Tim
and the children and staff at
St George's Hospital.

Senior editor Elinor Greenwood
Senior art editor Jacqueline Gooden
Traditional stories retold by Lorrie Mack
Editorial assistant Fleur Star

Publishing manager Susan Leonard
Managing art editor Clare Shedden
Picture researcher Harriet Mills
Production Lloyd Robertson
and Emma Hughes
DTP designer Almudena Díaz

First published in Great Britain in 2004
by Dorling Kindersley Limited
80 Strand, London WC2R ORL

A Penguin Company

10 9 8 7 6 5 4 3 2 1

Copyright © 2004 Dorling Kindersley Limited, London
First paperback edition 2005

A CIP catalogue record for this book
is available from the British Library.

Paperback edition ISBN 1-4053-1382-X
Hardback edition ISBN 1-4053-0707-2

Colour reproduction by Colourscan, Singapore

Printed and bound in China by
Toppan Printing Co., Ltd

Discover more at
www.dk.com

Contents

Foreword

THIS BOOK IS A COLLECTION OF MAGICAL, exciting, fun, happy and even scary tales, but it is more than that. It is a way of helping to raise funds for the Paediatric Intensive Care Unit at St George's Hospital in London. Visitors to this special ward see bravery from the children; dedication by the staff; love from the parents and carers; and magical moments when a child recovers. I know this because, in 2002, my little boy Archie was treated at St George's for a serious brain virus. Without the help of the doctors, nurses and support staff we wouldn't have our gorgeous little boy with us today.

My husband Tim, my family and I spent many hours reading to Archie while he was unconscious in the hope that he might be able to hear us. During these long hours, I began thinking about putting together a different kind of bedtime story book – one with a unique mix of stories and poems, chosen by talented stars, with a fantastic CD to go with it. And now, here's the book I dreamt about – *Stars at Bedtime*!

Reading a story to your children, safe in the knowledge they will fall asleep happy and healthy is a real privilege; for most of us it's that moment when calm arrives and all is right with the world.

We hope that you will enjoy these stories, knowing that you have helped so many children and families.

Thank you.

Victoria Chilcott

4

Pete Waterman

"I have always been interested in trains and grew up listening to Thomas stories. They can stimulate a hunger for knowledge about real engines and every story has a moral that makes perfect sense to me."

The world of the Rev. W. Awdry

Wilbert Awdry's interest in railways began when he was a child living in Box, Wiltshire. He used to lie awake in bed listening to the trains nearby and imagine they were talking to each other. Later he made up train stories to tell his young son Christopher when he was ill. Awdry's first book was published in 1945.

Thomas the Tank Engine
Thomas and the Guard
by The Rev. W. Awdry
illustrated by C. Reginald Dalby

THOMAS the Tank Engine is very proud of his branch line. He thinks it is the most important part of the whole railway.

He has two coaches. They are old, and need new paint, but he loves them very much. He calls them Annie and Clarabel. Annie can only take passengers, but Clarabel can take passengers, luggage and the Guard.

As they run backwards and forwards along the line, Thomas sings them little songs, and Annie and Clarabel sing too.

When Thomas starts from a station he sings,
"Oh, come along! We're rather late. Oh, come along! We're rather late."
And the coaches sing, "We're coming along, we're coming along."

They don't mind what Thomas says to them because they know he is trying to please the Fat Controller;

and they know, too, that if Thomas is cross, he is not cross with them. He is cross with the engines on the Main Line who have made him late.

The real Thomas
C. Reginald Dalby, Thomas's original illustrator, based his figures on both Rev. Awdry's original sketches and real British steam engines. The model for Thomas himself was an obscure 0-6-0T Class E2 shunting engine built in the Victorian era for the London, Brighton, and South Coast Railway.

One day they had to wait for Henry's train. It was late. Thomas was getting crosser and crosser. "How can I run my line properly if Henry is always late? He doesn't realize that the Fat Controller depends on ME," and he whistled impatiently.

At last Henry came.

"Where have you been, lazybones?" asked Thomas crossly.

"Oh dear, my system is out of order; no one understands my case. You don't know what I suffer," moaned Henry.

"Rubbish!" said Thomas, "you're too fat; you need exercise!"

Lots of people with piles of luggage got out of Henry's train, and they all climbed into Annie and Clarabel. Thomas had to wait till they were ready. At last the Guard blew his whistle, and Thomas started at once.

6

The Guard turned round to jump into his van, tripped over an old lady's umbrella, and fell flat on his face.

By the time he had picked himself up, Thomas and Annie and Clarabel were steaming out of the station.

"Come along! Come along!"

puffed Thomas, but Clarabel didn't want to come. "I've lost my nice Guard, I've lost my nice Guard," she sobbed. Annie tried to tell Thomas "We haven't a Guard, we haven't a Guard," but he was hurrying, and wouldn't listen.

"Oh, come along! Oh, come along!"

he puffed impatiently.

Birth of a classic

It was Wilbert Awdry's wife who first encouraged him to find a publisher for his railway tales. When he followed her advice, the manuscript was demanded so quickly that he had no time to prepare a neat copy, and ended up submitting the original scraps of paper on which he'd jotted the stories and sketches down.

Annie and Clarabel tried to put on their brakes, but they couldn't without the Guard.

"Where is our Guard? Where is our Guard?" they cried. Thomas didn't stop till they came to a signal.

"Bother that signal!" said Thomas. "What's the matter?" "I don't know," said his Driver. "The Guard will tell us in a minute." They waited and waited, but the Guard didn't come.

"Peep peep peep peep! Where is the Guard?" whistled Thomas.

"We've left him behind," sobbed Annie and Clarabel together. The Driver, the Fireman, and the passengers looked, and there was the Guard running as fast as he could along the line, with his flags in one hand and his whistle in the other.

Everybody cheered him. He was very hot, so he sat down and had a drink and told them all about it.

"I'm very sorry, Mr Guard," said Thomas.

"It wasn't your fault, Thomas; it was the old lady's umbrella. Look, the signal is down; let's make up for lost time."

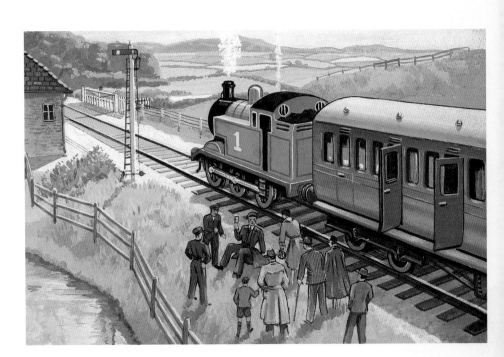

Annie and Clarabel were so pleased to have their Guard again, that they sang, "As fast as you like, as fast as you like!" to Thomas, all the way, and they reached the end of the line quicker than ever before.

8

Kate Winslet

"The illustrations are fantastic – very imaginative and educational – and it has the most wonderful last line I have ever read in a story."

Setting the scene

This illustrated poem takes a child's-eye view of the world. Here is a selection of verses from it, including the book's final verse.

The world of Marion Dane Bauer

American author Marion Dane Bauer was a teacher before she married and had two children. Later, she became a foster carer and took in exchange students. Since she became a writer, she has produced more than 30 books for young people, including readers, novels, and guides as well as picture books like this.

Why Do Kittens Purr?
by Marion Dane Bauer
illustrated by Henry Cole

Five important questions . . .

Why do spiders spin?
To make a plate
to keep their dinner in.

Why do mice squeak?
To say, "I'm shy.
Please, don't peek!"

because! . . . So why do bees buzz? Just because! . . . So why do bees buzz? Just because! . . . So why do

9

What makes frogs
hop, hop, hop?
They can't stop, stop, stop.

So why do bees buzz?
Just because!

And why does the sun come
back when night is through?
To see you.
To see you!

Stephen Fry

"Because Paddington
   has dignity.
Because he is a bear.
Because he likes
   marmalade sandwiches.
Because he is helpful.
Because he has problems
   with tidiness."

Setting the Scene

First published in 1958,
A Bear Called Paddington
was so popular that
a whole series of
Paddington stories
followed. Their author
Michael Bond was
rewarded with an
OBE in 1997. In this
picture-book version
of the original story,
we learn how Paddington
came to be adopted by
the Brown family.

Paddington Bear
by *Michael Bond*
illustrated by *R.W. Alley*

Paddington finds a home . . .

Mr AND MRS BROWN first met Paddington on a railway platform. In fact, that was how he came to have such an unusual name for a bear, because Paddington was the name of the station.

The Browns were waiting to meet their daughter, Judy, when Mr Brown noticed something small and furry half hidden behind some bicycles. "It looks like a bear," he said.

"A bear?" repeated Mrs Brown. "In Paddington station? Don't be silly, Henry. There can't be!"

But Mr Brown was right. It was sitting on an old leather

suitcase marked **WANTED ON VOYAGE,** and as they drew near it stood up and politely raised its hat.

"Good afternoon," it said. "May I help you?"

"That's very kind of you," said Mr Brown, "but as a matter of fact, we were wondering if we could help *you*?"

"You're a very small bear to be all alone in a station," said Mrs Brown. "Where are you from?"
The bear looked around carefully before replying.

this bear. Thank you . . . Please look after this bear. Thank you . . . Please look after this bear. Thank you

11

"Darkest Peru. I'm not really supposed to be here at all. I'm a stowaway."

"You don't mean to say you've come all the way from South America by yourself?" exclaimed Mrs Brown. "Whatever did you do for food?"

Unlocking the suitcase with a small key, the bear took out an almost empty glass jar. "I ate marmalade," it said. "Bears like marmalade."

Mrs Brown took a closer look at the label around the bear's neck. It said, quite simply,

PLEASE LOOK AFTER THIS BEAR.

THANK YOU.

"Oh Henry!" she cried. "We can't just leave him here. There's no knowing what might happen to him. Can't he come home and stay with us?"

"Stay with us?" repeated Mr Brown nervously.
He looked down at the bear. "Er, would you like that?" he asked. "That is," he added hastily, "if you have nothing else planned".

"Oooh, yes," replied the bear. "I would like that very much. I've nowhere to go and everyone seems in such a hurry."

"That settles it," said Mrs Brown. "Now, you must be thirsty after your journey. Mr Brown will buy you a nice cup of tea while I go and meet our daughter, Judy."
"But, Mary," said Mr Brown. "We don't even know his name".
Mrs Brown thought for a moment. "I know," she said. "We can call him Paddington! After the station."
"Paddington!" The bear tested it several times to make sure. "It sounds very important."

12

Mr Brown tried it out next. "Follow me, Paddington," he said. "I'll take you to the restaurant."

Paddington had never been inside a restaurant before, and he was very excited when he saw what Mr Brown had bought him.

He was so hungry and thirsty he didn't know which to do first – eat or drink. "I think I'll try both at the same time, if you don't mind," he announced.

Without waiting for a reply, he climbed up onto the table and promptly stepped on a large cream and jam cake.

Mr Brown stared out of the window, pretending he had tea with a bear in Paddington station every day of his life.

"Henry!" cried Mrs Brown, when she arrived with Judy. "What are you doing to that poor bear? He's covered in jam and cream."

Bear in boots
The shiny red boots associated with Paddington were first added by the makers of the popular Paddington Bear toy. Later, Michael Bond wrote them into his stories.

Paddington jumped up to raise his hat. In his haste, he slipped on a patch of strawberry jam and fell over backwards into his cup of tea. "I think we'd better go before anything else happens," said Mr Brown.

Judy took hold of Paddington's paw. "Come along," she said. "We'll take you home and you can meet Mrs Bird and my brother, Jonathan."

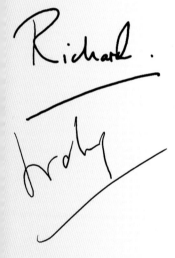

"All our children loved this story about a little boy who dreams of a magic land where he is king. We both found the tale and the illustrations as enchanting as the kids did."

Richard .

Judy

Setting the Scene

When Max is sent to bed without supper, he imagines himself in the fantastic land of the wild things. American author and illustrator Maurice Sendak based his 1963 creations on the eccentric relatives who terrified him as a child with their claims that he was "so cute I could eat you up".

Where the Wild Things Are
by *Maurice Sendak*

Max arrives in a strange land . . .

And when he came to the place where the wild things are
they roared their terrible roars and gnashed their terrible teeth
and rolled their terrible eyes and showed their terrible claws

till Max said **"BE STILL!"**
and tamed them with the magic trick
of staring into all their yellow eyes without blinking once
and they were frightened and called him the most wild thing of all

and made him king of all wild things.
"And now," cried Max, "let the wild rumpus start!"

13

14

Richard Curtis

"This children's story has a cracking plot. I have to confess, I've never got through reading it aloud without getting a tear in my eye. Author Giles Andreae is a friend of mine and I always feel he writes with love, care, and compassion."

Setting the Scene

These few verses introduce the story of young Leo, who is not the same as other lions; what he wants most of all in the world is "a hug and a nuzzle or two".

The Lion Who Wanted to Love

by Giles Andreae illustrated by David Wojtowycz

Leo explains how he feels . . .

Deep in the African heartland
Way out on the hot sunny plains,
There lived a small lion who didn't fit in
And Leo was this lion's name.

Now lions are usually fierce
And lions are meant to be strong,
But Leo just wanted to love everybody
And play with his friends all day long.

"You worry me, Leo, my darling,"
His mum started saying one day.
"You'll never survive in the animal world
If you don't learn to hunt for your prey."

"But, Mummy," said Leo, bewildered,
"I don't think I quite understand.
I'm sure there are plenty of lions that hunt
Who could kill all the beasts in the land."

"And besides, when I'm close to a zebra
A funny thought goes through my head,
Instead of deciding to bite through his skin
I'd much rather hug him instead."

Kate Thornton

"The Three Little Pigs is a great story — it's also very scary when you're little, which is one of the main reasons why I loved it as a child!"

Kate Thornton

Did you know?

★ Like most traditional stories, this one has several different versions. In some, the first two pigs survive and go to live with their brother in the brick house.

In others, the wolf kidnaps the first two pigs, and the third one rescues them.

One particularly nasty variation has the third pig cutting open the wolf's belly to let his brothers out.

The Three Little Pigs
illustrated by Paul Howard

THE THREE LITTLE PIGS lived together with their mother. The family was poor, and the house was too small, so one day the little pigs' mother said, "You are all old enough to go and build your own houses".

The three little pigs said goodbye to their mother and set off. "Look out for the big bad wolf!" she called after them.

The first little pig built a house out of straw. He had just finished when the big, bad wolf came visiting.

"Little pig, little pig, let me come in," he growled.

The frightened little pig replied, "No, not by the hair of my chinny chin chin".

The wolf roared, "Then I'll *huff* and I'll *puff* and I'll blow your house in".

So he huffed and he puffed and he blew the house of straw to bits. The wolf ate up the first little pig.

The second little pig built a house out of sticks. The very next day, the big, bad wolf came visiting. "Little pig, little pig, let me come in," he growled.

The scared little pig replied, "No, not by the hair of my chinny chin chin".
The wolf roared, "Then I'll *huff* and I'll *puff* and I'll blow your house in".

So he huffed and he puffed and he blew the house of sticks to bits.
The wolf ate up the second little pig.

The third little pig built a house out of bricks. The big, bad wolf came, as he had to the other little pigs, and said:

"Little pig, little pig, let me come in."

"No, not by the hair of my chinny chin chin," the little pig replied.

The wolf roared, "Then I'll *huff* and I'll *puff* and I'll blow your house in".

Well, the wolf huffed and he puffed, and he huffed and he puffed and he puffed and he huffed, but he could **NOT** get the house down. He became very angry.

"Right!" he howled. "You won't get away from me. I am going to come down the chimney!" and he clambered up the side of the house onto the roof.

The third little pig thought quickly. He rushed to fill a pot with water and made up a blazing fire beneath. Just as the water in the pot began to boil, the wolf slithered down the chimney, SPLASH! straight into the pot. The little pig slammed down the lid, boiled him up, and ate the big, bad wolf for dinner.

18

Martin Clunes

"I love this book because of the way the drawings capture the essence of dogs so well and having the story in verse makes it all the more memorable."

Hairy Maclary from Donaldson's Dairy
by Lynley Dodd

OUT OF THE GATE
and off for a walk
went Hairy Maclary
from Donaldson's Dairy

and Hercules Morse
as big as a horse

with Hairy Maclary
from Donaldson's Dairy.

Bottomley Potts
covered in spots,
Hercules Morse
as big as a horse

and Hairy Maclary
from Donaldson's Dairy.

Muffin McLay
like a bundle of hay,
Bottomley Potts
covered in spots,
Hercules Morse
as big as a horse

and Hairy Maclary
from Donaldson's Dairy.

Bitzer Maloney
all skinny and bony,
Muffin McLay
like a bundle of hay,
Bottomley Potts
covered in spots,
Hercules Morse
as big as a horse

and Hairy Maclary
from Donaldson's Dairy.

Schnitzel von Krumm
with a very low tum,
Bitzer Maloney
all skinny and bony,
Muffin McLay
like a bundle of hay,
Bottomley Potts
covered in spots,
Hercules Morse
as big as a horse

and Hairy Maclary
from Donaldson's Dairy.

With tails in the air
they trotted on down
past the shops and the park
to the far end of town.
They sniffed at the smells
and they snooped at each door,
when suddenly,
out of the shadows
they
saw ...

SCARFACE CLAW
The toughest Tom
in
town.

"EEEEEOWWWFFTZ!"
said Scarface Claw.

Off with a yowl
a wail and a howl,
a scatter of paws
and a clatter of claws,
went Schnitzel von Krumm
with a very low tum,
Bitzer Maloney
all skinny and bony,
Muffin McLay
like a bundle of hay,
Bottomley Potts
covered in spots,
Hercules Morse
as big as a horse

and Hairy Maclary
from Donaldson's Dairy,

straight back home to bed.

20

Annie Lennox

"My daughter and I love to read together, and I've chosen this story because it's her very favourite."

Setting the scene

It's mid-winter in Brambly Hedge and the mice who live there have woken up to a thick covering of snow. There hasn't been snow like this for years and the mice decide to hold a Snow Ball. They set about the preparations for the party.

Did you know?

⭐ The Brambly Hedge stories have inspired a vast and varied collection of related merchandise. There are Brambly Hedge stuffed toys, sets of china, cross-stitch kits, resin and pewter figures, stationery ranges, ceramic tableaux, clocks, jigsaws, wallpaper, paperweights, crystal, storage tins, and much, much more.

Winter Story
by Jill Barklem
The Brambly Hedge mice plan a party ...

THERE WAS A DEEP drift of snow banked against the Store Stump and the elder mice, after discussion, declared it to be "just right" for the Ice Hall. Mr Apple dug the first tunnel to check that the snow was firm.

"It's perfect!" he called back from the middle of the drift. The mice picked up their shovels and the digging began.

The snow was dug from inside the drift, piled into carts and taken down to the stream. Wilfred and Teasel helped enthusiastically, but they were sent home again when Mr Apple caught them putting icicles down Catkin's dress.

The middle of the drift was carefully hollowed out. Mr Apple inspected the roof very thoroughly to make sure that it was safe.
"Safe as the Store Stump!" he declared.

All the kitchens along Brambly Hedge were warm and busy. Hot soups, punches and puddings bubbled and in the ovens pies browned and sizzled. Clover and Catkin helped Mrs Apple string crabapples to roast over the fire. The boys had to sit and watch because they ate too many.

"It's not that I mind, dears, but we must have SOME left for the punch!"

The Glow-worms were put in charge of the lighting. Toadflax fetched them early from the bank at the end of the Hedge, for Mrs Apple had insisted that they should have a good supper before their long night's work began.

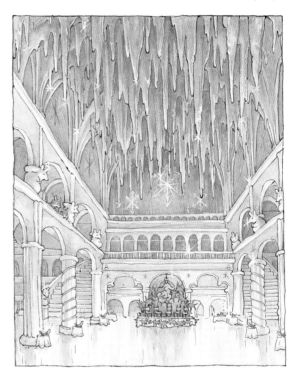

By tea-time the Hall was finished. The ice columns and carvings sparkled in the blue-green light and the polished dance floor shone. Tables were set at the end of the Hall and eager cooks bustled in from their kitchens with baskets of food.

The children decorated a small raised platform with sprays of holly while Basil, the keeper of the hedgerow vines, set out some chairs for the musicians. When all was done, the mice admired their handiwork and went home to wash and change.

As muffs and mufflers were left at the door, it was clear that all the mice had dressed up for the grand occasion. Wilfred and Teasel crept under a table to watch and every now and then a little paw appeared and a cream cake disappeared.

Basil struck up a jolly tune on his violin and the dancing began. All the dances were very fast and twirly and were made even faster by the slippery ice floor. Wilfred and Teasel whirled their sisters round so quickly that their paws left the ground.

"I don't feel very well," said Clover, looking rather green.

Mrs Apple stood on a chair and banged two saucepan lids together.

"Supper is served," she called.

The eating and drinking and dancing carried on late into the night. At midnight, all the hedgerow children were taken home to bed.

22

Lorraine Kelly

"I find the idea that only a real princess is so delicate very funny. And after all, every little girl wants to be a princess!"

Lorraine Kelly

The world of Hans Christian Andersen

Born in Denmark in 1805, Hans Andersen was a homely, awkward boy who took refuge in stories and music. When he was 14, he went to Copenhagen to seek success on the stage. He failed miserably, but went on to achieve immortality as a writer. Unlike most of his stories, which were entirely original, *The Princess and the Pea* is based on an earlier folk tale.

The Princess and the Pea
by Hans Christian Andersen
illustrated by Julie Downing

ONCE THERE WAS A DASHING PRINCE. More than anything, he wanted to marry a beautiful princess so he travelled to every corner of the world to look for one. Wherever he went, would-be brides were brought before him. Most of them were beautiful and all of them claimed to be real princesses. But the prince always felt there was something wrong – he didn't believe they were of true royal blood.

Feeling very sad, he returned home. One evening not long after, there was a terrible storm – thunder banged, lightning flashed and rain pelted down. Suddenly, above the storm's roar, the prince and his family heard a knock on the palace door. When the king opened it, he found a shivering girl with water dripping from her hair and running out through her shoes.

"Come inside, my dear," he said gently. "Tell us who you are and why you are here."
"I am a princess who is lost in the storm," she said in a clear voice.

The prince's hopes stirred. Despite her bedraggled state, she was *very* beautiful, and he wanted *so* much to find a princess. "We'll know the truth soon enough," thought the queen, who disappeared to prepare a room for the visitor. First she took all the bedclothes off the bed and placed a tiny, hard pea on the mattress.

Then she ordered twenty more mattresses to be piled up, and twenty plump eiderdowns to be placed on top. When everything was ready, she left the weary princess to retire. In the morning, the royal family asked if she'd had a peaceful night.

"Oh no – it was horrible!" she wailed. "I didn't get a wink of sleep. There was something small and hard in the bed and it's left me black and blue all over."

Instantly, the queen knew her son had found his bride: only a real princess has skin so delicate that she can feel a single pea through twenty mattresses and twenty eiderdowns. The prince and princess lived together happily for a long long time and had lots of laughing children. As for the pea, it's displayed in the royal museum, where you can go and see it for yourself.

24

Carol Smillie

"This book makes me laugh out loud every time I read it. The illustrations are hilarious and imaginatively drawn. I read a lot of children's books to my children, but Clarice Bean is a breath of fresh air with something for everyone."

Setting the scene

British writer and illustrator Lauren Child created Clarice Bean on her first visit to New York when she was in her mid 20s. *Clarice Bean, That's Me* introduces us to Clarice, her family, her thoughts, and her adventures.

Clarice Bean That's Me
by Lauren Child

When I get a bee in my bonnet and Mum needs some peace and quiet she says,

Go and run about in the garden.

This usually does the trick.

Sometimes I chuck potatoes over next door's wall.

Because I might want to be an acrobat I have to keep nimble and flexible. I do this by scrinching into the laundry basket.

Getting out is the tricky bit.

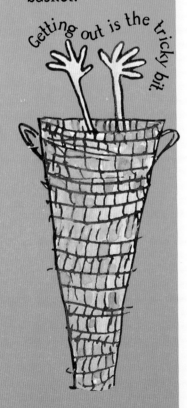

I do **b a l a n c i n g** and smiling in tights.

(That's a very important part of acrobatics.)

26

Alan Titchmarsh

"When I was a little boy,
I loved animals as much
as I loved gardens, so
The Tale of Peter Rabbit
was the perfect story
for me."

The world of Beatrix Potter

Born in 1866, Beatrix Potter lived in London but spent her early summers in the country with her parents. She believed that "the town child is more alive to the fresh beauty of the country than a child who is country born". Her pictures and stories have been enchanting children for over 100 years.

ABRIDGED VERSION

The Tale of Peter Rabbit
by Beatrix Potter

ONCE UPON A TIME, there were four little rabbits, and their names were Flopsy, Mopsy, Cotton-tail, and Peter.

"Now, my dears," said old Mrs. Rabbit one morning, "you may go into the fields or down the lane, but don't go into Mr. McGregor's garden. "Now run along, and don't get into mischief. I am going out."

Then old Mrs. Rabbit took a basket and her umbrella, and went through the woods to the baker's. She bought a loaf of brown bread and five currant buns.

Flopsy, Mopsy, and Cotton-tail, who were good little bunnies, went down the lane to gather blackberries. But Peter, who was very naughty, ran straight away to Mr. McGregor's garden, and squeezed under the gate! First he ate some lettuces and some French beans, and then he ate some radishes. And then, feeling rather sick, he went to look for some parsley.

But round the end of a cucumber frame,
whom should Peter meet but Mr. McGregor!
Mr. McGregor jumped up and ran after
Peter, waving a rake and calling out, "Stop
thief!" Peter was most dreadfully frightened;
he rushed all over the garden, for he had
forgotten the way back to the gate.

He lost one of his shoes among the cabbages,
and the other shoe amongst the potatoes. He ran
into a gooseberry net, and
got caught by the large
brass buttons on his jacket.

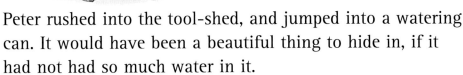

Mr. McGregor came up with a
sieve, which he intended to pop
upon the top of Peter; but Peter
wriggled out just in time, leaving
his jacket behind him.

Peter rushed into the tool-shed, and jumped into a watering
can. It would have been a beautiful thing to hide in, if it
had not had so much water in it.

Mr. McGregor was quite sure that Peter was
somewhere in the tool-shed, perhaps hidden
underneath a flower pot. He began to turn
them over carefully, looking under each.

Suddenly, Peter sneezed – "Kertyschoo!"
Mr. McGregor was after him in no time.
He tried to put his foot upon Peter, who
jumped out of a window, upsetting three plants.
The window was too small for Mr. McGregor,
and he was tired of running after Peter.
He went back to his work.

28

Life drawing
Throughout her childhood, Beatrix Potter loved drawing plants and animals. Every time she returned to London, she brought live creatures with her to use as models. At different times, these included rabbits, mice, a white rat, and a hedgehog she described as "a charming little creature".

Peter sat down to rest; he was out of breath and trembling with fright, and he had not the least idea which way to go. Also he was very damp with sitting in that watering can. After a time he began to wander about, going lippity–lippity – not very fast. He tried to find his way out of the garden, but he became more and more puzzled.

Peter went back towards the tool-shed. Suddenly, quite close to him, he heard the sound of a hoe – scr-r-ritch, scratch, scratch, scritch. Peter climbed upon a wheelbarrow and peeped over. The first thing he saw was Mr. McGregor hoeing onions. His back was turned towards Peter, and beyond him was the gate!

Peter got down very quietly off the wheelbarrow, and started running as fast as he could go along a straight walk behind some blackcurrant bushes. Mr. McGregor caught sight of him at the corner, but Peter did not care. He slipped underneath the gate, and was safe at last in the wood outside the garden.

Peter never stopped running or looked behind him till he got home.

He was so tired that he flopped down on the nice soft sand on the floor of the rabbit-hole and shut his eyes. He did not feel well. His mother put him to bed and gave him some camomile tea.

But Flopsy, Mopsy, and Cotton-tail had bread and milk and fresh blackberries for supper.

Did you know?

★ Peter Rabbit made his first appearance when Beatrix Potter was in her 20s. She used drawings of him to illustrate one of her letters to a small friend – a five-year-old boy called Noël Moore.

★ In her old age, Beatrix Potter bought a farm in the Lake District and became an expert sheep breeder.

Fearne Cotton

"I loved these poems when I was young and adored the illustrations of the flowers and the fairies."

fearne !
x ♡

The world of Cicely Mary Barker

Like Beatrix Potter, Cicely Mary Barker was born in London, and spent her childhood drawing and painting. In 1911, aged just 16, she sold the first of her famous flower paintings, which are not only charming, but perfect in every botanical detail. In all, there are eight *Flower Fairy* books; these two poems are from *Flower Fairies of the Garden*, and *Flower Fairies of the Trees* respectively.

Flower Fairies
by Cicely Mary Barker

Two songs . . .

The Song of the Geranium Fairy

Red, red, vermilion red,
With buds and blooms in a glorious head!
There isn't a flower, the wide world through,
That glows with a brighter scarlet hue.
Her name – Geranium – ev'ryone knows;
She's just as happy wherever she grows,
In an earthen pot or a garden bed –
Red, red, vermilion red.

The Song of the Red Clover Fairy

The Fairy: O, what a great big bee
Has come to visit me!
He's come to find my honey.
O, what a great big bee!

The Bee: O, what a great big Clover!
I'll search it well, all over,
And gather all its honey.
O, what a great big Clover!

30

Fiona Phillips

"I remember this story so well from my childhood, and now I'm enjoying it all over again with my four-year-old son Nat. It's one of his favourites too."

Fiona Phillips

Did you know?

★ Various versions of this folk-tale were common in European and English-speaking countries in the 19th century. The story's central figure was usually made from gingerbread, but a bun or cake of some kind was often involved instead, and the story was also known as *Johnny Cake*.

The Gingerbread Man
illustrated by Peter Bowman

ONCE UPON A TIME an old man and an old woman lived in a little old house. They had no children so one day the woman decided to make a boy out of gingerbread, with currant eyes and chocolate-drop buttons. When he was all ready, and as handsome as he could be, she put him in the oven to bake. "Now I'll have a child of my own," she said. She waited patiently, and when he was done, she opened the oven door.

Before she could stop him, the Gingerbread Man jumped onto the floor and ran out the door as fast as his legs would carry him. The old couple chased him down the path, but they couldn't run fast enough, and as he disappeared, they heard him sing,

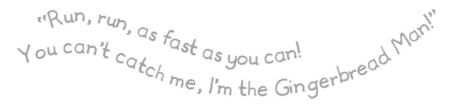

"Run, run, as fast as you can! You can't catch me, I'm the Gingerbread Man!"

He ran and ran, and soon he met a cow.
"Stop!" said the cow. "You look very good to eat."
But the Gingerbread Man just kept running, as he sang,

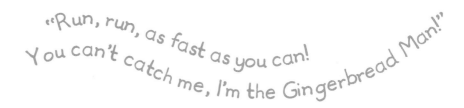

"Run, run, as fast as you can! You can't catch me, I'm the Gingerbread Man!"

can! You can't catch me, I'm the Gingerbread Man! . . Run, run, as fast as you can! You can't catch me,

31

Further down the road, the little man met a horse.
"Stop!" said the horse. "You look very good to eat."
Still, the Gingerbread Man kept running, and singing,

"Run, run, as fast as you can!
You can't catch me, I'm the Gingerbread Man!"

Warm tradition
Gingerbread has been baked in Europe for centuries, and historians think it may have been introduced by 11th-century Crusaders returning from the eastern Mediterranean. Whether the confection was dark or light, sweet or spicy, it was almost always cut into shapes: animals, stars, houses, hearts, flowers, or – of course – people. One early custom required unmarried ladies to eat gingerbread "husbands" to increase their chances of finding the real thing.

The Gingerbread Man ran faster and faster.
Soon, he met a sly old fox.
"Stop!" said the fox. "I want to talk to you."
But he didn't stop. He just sang,

"Run, run, as fast as you can!
You can't catch me, I'm the Gingerbread Man!"

But the fox could run fast too, so he
chased the little man to a river bank.
"Would you like to cross?" asked
the fox. "Then jump on my tail."
Halfway across, the fox called
out, "The water is deep – jump on my back!"
A little further on, the fox spoke again:
"It's deeper now – jump on my nose."

Just then they reached the other bank.
The fox opened his mouth wide,
and the Gingerbread Man fell in.

"Dear me," he cried, "I'm half gone!"
Then a moment later, "Oh no! I'm
all gone!" He never spoke again.

32

Neil Fox

"I've read this story many many times to my little girl Scarlet, who loves to hear how Little Bear falls asleep in Big Bear's lovely, reassuring, snuggly arms. Eventually, Scarlet nods off too . . . a heavenly moment for any parent!"

Setting the scene

Little Bear can't sleep. It's too dark! Big Bear has already brought him the tiniest lantern, and then a bigger lantern, and then the Biggest Lantern of Them All! But Little Bear still can't sleep.

Can't You Sleep, Little Bear?

by *Martin Waddell*
illustrated by *Barbara Firth*

Big Bear takes Little Bear outside . . .

LITTLE BEAR TRIED AND TRIED AND TRIED to go to sleep, but he couldn't.

"Can't you sleep, Little Bear?" groaned Big Bear, putting down his Bear Book (with just two pages to go) and padding over to the bed.

"I'm scared," said Little Bear.
"Why are you scared, Little Bear?" asked Big Bear.
"I don't like the dark," said Little Bear.
"What dark?" asked Big Bear.
"The dark all around us," said Little Bear.
"But I brought you the Biggest Lantern of Them All, and there isn't any dark left," said Big Bear.
"Yes, there is!" said Little Bear. "There is, out there!"
And he pointed out of the Bear Cave, at the night.

Big Bear saw that Little Bear was right. Big Bear was very puzzled. All the lanterns in the world couldn't light up the dark outside.

the dark! . . . But I'm scared of the dark! . . . But I'm scared of the dark! . . . But I'm scared of the dark! . . .

33

Big Bear thought about it for a long time, and then
he said, "Come on, Little Bear."

"Where are we going?" asked Little Bear.

"Out!" said Big Bear.

"Out into the darkness?" said Little Bear.

"Yes!" said Big Bear.

"But I'm scared of the dark!" said Little Bear.

"No need to be!" said Big Bear, and he took Little Bear
by the paw and led him out from the cave into the night

and it was ...

DARK!

"Ooooh! I'm scared,"
said Little Bear, cuddling
up to Big Bear.

Big Bear lifted Little Bear,
and cuddled him, and said,
"Look at the dark, Little Bear."
And Little Bear looked.

"I've brought you the moon,
Little Bear," said Big Bear.

"The bright yellow moon,
and all the twinkly stars."

But Little Bear didn't say
anything, for he had gone
to sleep, warm and safe in
Big Bear's arms.

Big Bear carried Little Bear back into
the Bear Cave, fast asleep, and he settled
down with Little Bear on one arm and the
Bear Book on the other, cosy in the Bear
Chair by the fire.

And Big Bear read the Bear Book right to ...

THE END

34

Sarah, The Duchess of York

"Little Red and her merry gang live in a magical world. They have all sorts of fun together and love to help others. When I was a little girl, I wanted to have a friend like Little Red. She's sweet and brave and funny and kind."

Sarah

Did you know?

★ Sarah Ferguson first sketched Little Red on a paper napkin as a logo for her American Charity, Chances for Children.

★ Little Blue, one of the other characters in the story, is the symbol of Sarah's international charity Children in Crisis.

Little Red
by Sarah, The Duchess of York
illustrated by Sam Williams

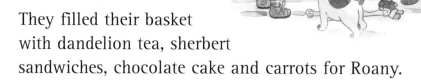

IT WAS A BEAUTIFUL SUNNY DAY. Little Red's cosy home nestled in the shade of Bluebell Wood.

Little Red, Little Blue, Roany the pony and Gino the dog busily prepared for their picnic at Lily Pad Pond.

They filled their basket with dandelion tea, sherbert sandwiches, chocolate cake and carrots for Roany.

Roany stood waiting impatiently with the wonky wooden wagon.
"I've been waiting for you forever and I'm getting hungry!" she snorted.
"Oh, Roany, you're always hungry!" said Little Red.
"All aboard!"
"What a buzz of a day!" Little Blue shouted.
"Perfect for a picnic!"

After a short while, they found a spot close to Lily Pad Pond. Little Red spread the blanket on the woodland floor and took out her tea set.
"Well, this *is* a nice spot."
The friends munched happily.

ABRIDGED VERSION

Suddenly they heard a **dreadful** noise.

SPLAT *SWOOSH* THWACK THUMP SQUEAK SPLOSH

"What was that?" whispered Little Red.
Little Blue trembled. "I don't like it here anymore.
Let's go back."
"Hold on!" Little Red said. "Don't you think we
should see what's going on?"
"Not really," said Roany.

SPLAT *SWOOSH* THWACK THUMP SQUEAK SPLOSH

"Come on, everyone! I am going to investigate. Anyone
care to join me?"
"Oh, all right!" Roany grumbled. "Let's get this over with."
Little Blue thought, *If they're going to go, I don't want to
be left behind.* The four friends all crept silently towards

the **dreadful** noise.

They peeked over the trunk of a fallen tree. There – in
the middle of the pond – a bunny floated on a lily pad.
An enormous heron shouted orders from the bank to an
army of frogs who were trying to tow the stranded bunny
to safety. "Left a bit! Get a move on!" he boomed.

"Can we help?" asked Little Red.
"Yes! Stop dithering and get over here. Chop, chop!"
thundered the heron. Quickly Little Red pulled out a rope.

"Tie one end around my bridle and throw one end
to the bunny. Hold tight, now!" Roany instructed. The
bunny nodded and she gripped the rope with all her might.

Slowly, and carefully, Roany
pulled the lily pad and
the bunny behind her.

A great ripple
of cheers rose up.
"Bravo! Good work!"
said the heron as he
clapped his giant wings together.

Little Red and Little Blue ran over to the bunny.
"Are you all right?" they asked. The bunny laughed.
"I jumped so far in the leapfrog competition with the
frogs that I couldn't get back!" she said, twitching
her nose. "Thank you for helping me."
"You're lucky you had brave picnickers around like me!"
Little Blue said. Roany groaned.

"Come on, everyone," said Little Red. "Let's have our picnic."
The friends sat down to eat. Roany even shared her
carrots with the bunny. And after everyone had eaten
to their heart's content, they spent a perfect afternoon
playing leapfrog.

The Cuckoo's Trick
from Atticus the Storyteller's 100 Greek Myths

by Lucy Coats illustrated by Anthony Lewis

Jerry Hall

Setting the scene

Atticus is on a long journey to the great Storytelling Festival near Troy. On his way, he stops to relate ancient Greek myths to anyone who'll listen. This is the 10th myth he passes on.

Did you know?

★ The oldest and most important temples of ancient Greece were dedicated to Hera. She appears in mythology thousands of years earlier than her husband Zeus.

ZEUS WAS BRAVE, HE WAS STRONG, HE WAS HANDSOME – in fact he was the greatest of the gods. So why wouldn't beautiful Hera marry him? He brought her magical flowers that bloomed a different colour each day. He brought her crowns made of moonbeams and necklaces made of starlight. But Hera just looked down her long straight perfect nose and laughed.

"Oh Zeus!" she sighed. "Just leave me alone and go and play with your thunderbolts. I'll never marry you until you can sit on my lap without me noticing – and that will be never!" And Zeus stomped back to his palace in a terrible temper that made the earth below shake and tremble.

Then he had an idea. He would do just what Hera had told him. He *would* go and play with his thunderbolts. Zeus stirred up the most tremendous thunderstorm that ever was. Then he changed himself into a cuckoo, and set out for Hera's palace through the storm. Wet, bedraggled and exhausted, he flew through the window of her bedroom, and landed shaking on her bed.

"Poor little cuckoo!" said Hera, stroking his soaking grey feathers. "Let me dry you." In no time at all the cuckoo was dry and comfortable, and nestling into Hera's lap. Then the cuckoo began to change. It grew and grew until – there was Zeus sitting in Hera's lap, laughing.

"Cuckoo!" he said, kissing her. "Will you marry me now?" And Hera had to agree.

Zeus and Hera were given many amazing wedding presents by all the gods and goddesses, in celebration of their marriage. The most wonderful gift of all was the magical apple tree given to Hera by Mother Earth. Its fruit was as golden as the sun, and it gave everlasting life to anyone who ate it. Hera planted it in her special garden, and set three beautiful nymphs to guard it, together with Argos, the hundred-eyed monster who never slept. In later times Heracles, the bravest hero of all, stole some of the precious apples, but that is quite another story.

38

Jack Dee

"The Emperor's New Clothes is a very funny tale about how people are so afraid of looking foolish that their common sense deserts them. In the story, a small child is the only one who sees clearly."

Did you know?

★ Hans Andersen wanted his stories to appeal to readers of all ages. His first collection was published as *Tales Told for Children*, but later in his life, he insisted that all references to children be dropped from the titles of his books.

The Emperor's New Clothes
by Hans Christian Andersen
illustrated by Philip Gough

THERE ONCE WAS AN EMPEROR who loved dressing up. He didn't care about winning battles, passing laws, or even seeing his people – except when he wanted to display his finery.

One day a pair of tricksters appeared at court. Knowing the Emperor's weakness, they claimed to be weavers. "Our cloth, Your Majesty, is not only beautiful, it is magic – only wise men can see it."

Very impressed, the Emperor vowed to have one of their suits. In it, he would not only look magnificent, he would be able to tell which of his subjects were wise men, and which were fools.

He gave the rogues piles of gold and put them to work. Soon they had set up two looms, and ordered bales of silk thread, which they kept for themselves. Then, they pretended to weave, waving their arms above empty machines.

Before long, the Emperor was anxious to know how they were getting on. He was certain, of course, that he would be able to see the magic cloth, but all the same, he decided to send his Senior Minister to investigate. When the honest old man arrived, he peered closely at the looms – but he could see nothing, because there was nothing there. The weavers exclaimed, "Aren't the patterns exquisite?" "Aren't the colours ravishing?"

Afraid to look foolish, he replied, "Ah yes.
I will tell the King!"
So the imposters carried on. Eventually, they pretended
to lay the cloth flat, they cut the air with tailors' scissors,
and they stitched away with empty needles. At last they
announced, "It is ready!"

As the Emperor arrived, the men held out their arms.
"Your Majesty," they said, "here is your new suit".
They slipped it on him, and wiggled their fingers
where the fastenings would have been. When he
was ready, he decided to walk through the streets
so his people could admire him.

"Fabulous!" "Elegant!" they exclaimed.

Nobody would admit there were no clothes to see.
Suddenly, a child's voice cried out, "The Emperor
has nothing on!" Soon, everyone was shouting,
"The Emperor has nothing on!" Finally, the truth
dawned on the Emperor himself, but he didn't want
to ruin the procession. So, bare naked, he marched
even more proudly, and his footmen held a
train that wasn't there.

40

Davina McCall

"I love this story as there is plenty of opportunity to make silly noises like 'wheee, wheee, wheeee!'. Plus there is so much detail in the pictures to talk about with the kids that the story really comes alive. The mice are very cute too!"

Davina xx

Setting the scene

Little Mouse has been kept awake by scary noises all night. He has asked to get into bed with Big Mouse four times, but Big Mouse won't let him. He says Little Mouse is too wriggly and his paws are cold.

The Very Noisy Night
by Diana Hendry
illustrated by Jane Chapman

Big Mouse gives in . . .

LITTLE MOUSE LAY AND LISTENED TO THE WIND huffing and puffing, the branch tap-tapping, and the owl hooting. And just as he was beginning to feel very sleepy indeed, he heard...

"WHEEe, WHEEe, WHEEEEe!"

"Big Mouse! Big Mouse!" he called. "You're snoring."

Wearily Big Mouse got up. He put his ear-muffs on Little Mouse's ears. He put a paper-clip on his own nose, and he went back to bed.

Little Mouse lay and listened to — **Nothing!**
It was very, very, very quiet. He couldn't hear the wind huffing or the branch tapping or the owl hooting or Big Mouse snoring. It was so quiet that Little Mouse felt he was all alone in the world.

He took off the ear-muffs. He got out of bed and pulled the paper-clip off Big Mouse's nose. "Big Mouse! Big Mouse!" he cried, "I'm lonely!"

Big Mouse flung back his blanket. "Better come into my bed," he said. So Little Mouse hopped in and his paws were cold...

And he needed a little wriggle before he fell fast asleep.

Big Mouse lay and listened to the wind huffing and puffing and the branch tapping and the owl hooting and Little Mouse snuffling, and very soon he heard the birds waking up. But neither of them heard the alarm clock...

BECAUSE THEY WERE BOTH FAST ASLEEP!

42

Chris Tarrant

"I was captivated by this story as a little boy, and it's great to see how much my kids love it now."

Telling tales

Like many other traditional tales, Hansel and Gretel existed in many different versions long before it was written down formally. The Grimm brothers first heard it from a family friend called Dortchen Wild, who later married Wilhelm.

Hansel and Gretel
by Jacob and Wilhelm Grimm
illustrated by Claire Pound

Long ago, two children called Hansel and Gretel lived near a large forest with their father, a poor woodcutter, and their stepmother. One year, famine came to their land and the family had only a single loaf of bread left to live on. "Soon we will starve!" cried the woodcutter's wife. "Tomorrow, we must take the children into the woods and leave them there. Then we will have only ourselves to feed."

The woodcutter loved his children dearly, but his wife tormented him until he agreed. Hansel and Gretel, however, had overheard the plan. "Don't worry," said Hansel. "I will keep us safe."

That night, Hansel crept outside and filled his pockets with white pebbles. Next morning, as the family walked into the forest, he kept falling behind. "Hurry up!" his father shouted. "I'm saying goodbye to my cat," said the boy. But really, he was dropping a trail of pebbles behind him.

When they reached a small clearing, the woodcutter said, "Wait here. We will come back for you".

The children waited and waited, but their parents never came. So, when night fell, they used Hansel's pebbles shining in the moonlight to lead the way home. The woodcutter was very glad to see them, but their stepmother was very cross. "Wicked children!" she shouted. "You must have wandered off."

Sometime later, the family fell on lean times again. Again, the woodcutter's wife made her plan, and again Hansel and Gretel overheard. But when Hansel tried to go outside to collect his pebbles, the door was locked – his stepmother had guessed what he was up to.

In the morning, their stepmother gave each child a crust of bread. "Here is your dinner," she said. So this time, as they walked through the forest, Hansel dropped crumbs behind him. As before, the woodcutter and his wife took the children to a clearing and left them.

Hansel was not worried, though – he thought his trail would lead them home. But later, when he tried to follow the crumbs, he saw that they'd been eaten by birds. Now frightened and hungry, Hansel and Gretel stumbled through the woods. After a long while, they found a magical cottage made of gingerbread and biscuits.

44

Just as they began to nibble,
an old woman appeared.
"Do come inside," she said.
"I'll make you a delicious supper
and put you to sleep in cosy beds."
But the old woman was really a
witch who lured children to her
house so she could eat them.
The next day, she put her plan
into operation. Hansel was too
thin for her liking, so she
locked him in a little cage
so she could feed him up and
make him plump and tasty.

That evening, before she cooked Hansel's dinner, she
ordered Gretel to test the oven. "Put your head inside!"

"How?" said Gretel, who was really quite clever.

"Stupid goose!" said the witch.
"Watch me." With that, she stuck her own
head in the oven. Instantly, Gretel pushed
her into the flames and shut the door.

Once the witch was dead, Hansel and
Gretel searched her cottage and
found gold and jewels, so they
stuffed them in their pockets
and set off the way they had
come. Eventually, the trees
began to look familiar,
and they knew they
were almost home.

When they arrived,
their father was alone
– his wicked wife had
gone. Overjoyed, and rich
beyond dreams, they all lived in
happiness for the rest of their lives.

Alfie's New School

by Jenny Eclair
illustrated by Pilar Morales

'Alfie's New School was inspired by the fact that, when I was a child, my dad was in the army so I had to change schools several times. I still remember the gut-wrenching embarrassment of every 'first day' — the feeling of being an outsider and everyone staring and not knowing who to sit next to at lunch time."

Jenny Eclair xxx

ALFIE WAS GOING TO A NEW SCHOOL but he didn't want to go. The old one had been alright. They did pink custard on sponge cake with hundreds and thousands. At his old school he didn't have a uniform, he just wore his Pikachu tee-shirt and his favourite red jumper.

Now he was all **"gussied up"**- that was the word his Granddad had used. It made him feel like he was wearing one of his sister's party frocks. His new white shirt felt tight around his neck and his grey shorts were itchy.

"Come on, Alfie, it's nearly time!" Oh no! His mother was standing at the front door and she was wearing a hat! It wasn't a normal hat, it was a mad hat, like a flower pot complete with big felt flowers, and she was wearing that purple lipstick and the big coat with the tiger skin collar.

"Wait for me!" Oh, not her too! Alfie's sister was three and she wouldn't go out of the house without fairy wings and a wand. Now, it was worse than he imagined; she was wearing her all-in-one bunny-rabbit outfit and rainbow-coloured wellies. She picked up a glittery handbag, two dollies and what looked like a dog biscuit and stomped over to her mother.

Standing together, his mother and his sister looked like they were about to run away and join the circus, not just walk him the three streets to his new school. Alfie wondered whether he could dawdle far enough away from them for people to think he was a grown-up boy walking to school on his own.

There were two more things that were causing Alfie prickles of embarrassment – his Super Ted lunch box (too babyish – he wanted a Digimon one) and his horrible bobble hat (he was forced to wear it to fend off ear infections).
"You can borrow my Tellytubby box if you like," whispered Alicia, "and my diamond tiara, but only for one day".
"Thanks kid," said Alfie. He knew she meant well.

There was no going back now. Alfie pulled his bobble hat as far down as he possibly could, and kept his eyes on the pavement. After a couple of streets, all of a sudden, Alicia sat down on the ground. "Tired! Me stay here!" pouted Alicia, and she rolled up in her bunny costume, shut her eyes, put her thumb in her mouth and fell fast asleep.

People were staring. They were trying not to, but they were. "Please, Alicia!" Alfie's mum was on her knees.

"Pleathe, Alithia!"

lisped Alfie through the gap where his front teeth used to be.

At that moment a woman wheeling an enormous pram stopped. She had to; otherwise Alicia would have been run over.
"Having trouble?" the woman with the pram asked. Alfie's mum said, "She won't walk any more, and we've got to get this one to school!"

"Well, how about hitching a ride on this wagon?"
said the woman. "We're heading in the same direction."
The woman had hair as orange as, well, oranges. She
picked up Alicia and sat her on the massive pram.
"There you go, my pet."

Bundled up in the pram were two very fat
baby twins with matching carroty hair and
dribbly chins. Alicia laughed. "Babies!"
she pointed.

"My horrible twin sisters," said a little voice.
Alfie looked around. There was a boy standing
behind the pram woman. He had red hair too.
"They're monsters," the boy added.
"I know the feeling," said Alfie, nodding at Alicia.
"'Least you've only got the one," the red-haired
boy sighed and then he added, "My name's Jake.
Are you going to Greendale Junior?"

"Yup!" replied Alfie.
"Me too," said Jake. "Do you
like peanut-butter sandwiches?"
"Yes," said Alfie. "I've got
Nutella".
"Swap ya," Jake grinned.
They were at the gates of
the school now. Alfie's mum
and Jake's mum were talking
like parrots.

Jake managed to dodge his mum when she swooped down
to kiss him. He started to run off and then he stopped.
"I'll go in with you, if you like... show you around."
"Thanks, Jake," said Alfie, and suddenly he wasn't scared.

He just shouted, **"Bye Mum!"** and off he went.

Sarah Brown

"The story of Greyfriars Bobby is one of friendship and loyalty, patience and persistence, grief and great longing. It's also a story about Edinburgh, where my son John was born. Gordon and I are looking forward to reading it to John one day, and taking him to see the statue."

Real-life hero

Greyfriars Bobby is a true story about a Skye terrior whose owner died in Edinburgh, Scotland in 1858. The faithful pet stayed by his master's body until he was found, and later followed the funeral procession to Greyfriars Churchyard. He remained near his owner's grave until his own death 14 years later.

THIS VERSION OF BOBBY'S STORY IS ADAPTED FROM THE PICTURE BOOK PUBLISHED BY ANDERSEN PRESS/RED FOX.

Greyfriars Bobby
by Ruth Brown

BECKY AND TOM WERE HOT AND THIRSTY. They had been sightseeing all day in Edinburgh. Suddenly, near the gates of a churchyard, Becky spied a drinking fountain.
"We're in luck," said Becky.
"Hey, looks like this fountain is for people *and* dogs," said Tom, reading the inscription:

A tribute to the affectionate fidelity of Greyfriars Bobby. In 1858 this dog followed the remains of his master to Greyfriars Churchyard and lingered near the spot until his death in 1872.

"Let's go in and see if we can find his master's grave," Tom suggested.

Becky and Tom went through the gates into the old churchyard, where they noticed a gardener at work.
"Maybe he knows more about Bobby," Becky suggested.

In fact, the gardener knew a great deal, and he was happy to talk to Becky and Tom. Right away, he showed them the grave they were looking for, and lingered there to tell Bobby's story.

"A hundred years ago, Bobby would lie right here in the sun. Sleeping soundly, he dreamt of the time before he lived in the churchyard. In those days, he used to help his master John Gray (known as Old Jock) to guard the cattle that were brought into the city each evening for market the following day.

"The story goes that, in the mornings, after work, Jock and Bobby would visit a café owned by Mrs Ramsay. She always saved titbits for Bobby – a bone, a bun or even a piece of pie. And on their rare days off they walked for miles in the hills where Jock had lived as a boy. But in the winter they stayed in the city, still guarding the cattle despite the freezing winds and bitter cold that eventually made Old Jock so ill that he died.

In memorium

Bobby is buried in Greyfriars Churchyard. The bronze statue of him and the fountain, which were erected in 1873, sit just outside the gates.

"Then, one grey morning, Bobby followed his master for the last time – to this place, Greyfriars Churchyard. He got as close as he could to Old Jock and that's where he stayed, huddled against the gravestone. But how cold and hungry he was that night!

"The next morning, Bobby found his way to the café hoping for a bit of food. He was welcomed with open arms, and when Mrs Ramsay found out where he was living, she fed him every day. In fact, a great many people were so touched by the little dog's loyalty that they helped to look after him.

Did you know?

★ After Bobby's master died, the Lord Provost of Edinburgh, Sir William Chambers, was so touched by the terrier's steadfast vigil that he arranged for his dog licence to be paid for by the city indefinitely.

"He was given his own engraved collar, and water bowl, and, best of all, official permission to live in this churchyard. He stayed for fourteen years until, finally, he was buried here too – near his beloved master, Old Jock."

"What a lovely story," said Becky.
"Aye," agreed the gardener. "Bobby never forgot his old friend".
"And I don't think we'll ever forget Bobby," declared Tom.

50

Richard E. Grant

"A boy who never grows up, and who can fly, fight pirates, and lose his shadow — Peter Pan is perfect for children. My first copy is one of my most treasured possessions."

Richard E. Grant

Setting the Scene

Peter Pan has invited the Darling children, Wendy, Michael, and John, to fly with him and the tiny fairy Tinker Bell from their nursery in London to Neverland – a place they have only seen in their dreams. For them the trip is a great adventure, but they don't realise how far they're going, or how long they'll be gone...

TEXT ADAPTED BY
MICHAEL JOHNSTONE

Peter Pan
by J.M. Barrie illustrated by Chris Molan
Flying to Neverland . . .

"SECOND TO THE RIGHT and straight on till morning." That, Peter told Wendy, was the way to Neverland. So great was the children's delight in flying that at first they wasted time circling round tall buildings that took their fancy.

Then they flew over the sea. Sometimes it was dark, and sometimes light, and now they were cold, and now they were too warm. When they were sleepy there was danger – for the moment they dropped off, down they fell.

Peter found this funny. "There he goes again," he would cry as Michael suddenly dropped like a stone. "Save him!" cried Wendy, and Peter would dive through the air and catch Michael just before he hit the sea.

The children could fly strongly now, though they still kicked far too much. If they saw a cloud in front of them, the more they tried to avoid it, the more certainly did they bump into it. Peter showed them how to lie out flat in the wind. This was so pleasant that they tried it several times, and found they could even go to sleep safely.

And so they drew near Neverland. And, after many moons, Peter cried out, "There it is!"

Wendy and John and Michael stood on tiptoe in the air to get their first sight of the island.
"There's a lagoon," said Wendy.
"Wendy, look at the mermaids!" said John.
"I can see the smoke of the Indian camp," said Michael.

It was getting darker. They huddled close to Peter, flying so low that sometimes a tree grazed their faces. Peter sent Tinker Bell off to see what was ahead.

"There's a pirate ship beneath us," Peter said. "Are there many pirates on the island?" asked John.
"Tons!"

"Who is captain of the pirates?"
"Hook!" answered Peter. "Captain James Hook. I cut off his right hand. He has an iron hook instead, and he claws with it. And you must promise me one thing." John paled. "If we meet Hook in open fight, you must leave him to me."

The world of J.M. Barrie

James Matthew Barrie was a Scottish writer who moved to London in 1885. He was inspired to write *Peter Pan* by a group of brothers he met in Hyde Park – the Llewelyn Davies boys.

Michael Llewelyn Davies in Peter Pan costume.

Be my Fwendy

The name Wendy, which was invented by Barrie, came from the affectionate greeting of a small child he knew. She tried to call him her "friendy", but "fwendy" was as close as she could get. The house the lost boys build in the story is the original Wendy House.

52

Jamie Oliver

"My mum used to read this to me when I was tiny, and now my daughter Poppy loves it too. We sing songs from the movie together and head off to bed with 'hi ho, hi ho!'"

Did you know?

★ In an early version of this traditional tale, the heroine was called Snowdrop, and the wicked Queen was forced to dance herself to death in red-hot slippers.

★ *Snow White*'s status as one of the best-known of all fairytales stems mainly from Walt Disney's 1937 film. And it's only in the film that the dwarfs have names: Happy, Dopey, Grumpy, Sneezy, Sleepy, Bashful, and Doc.

Snow White
by Jacob and Wilhelm Grimm
illustrated by Belinda Downes

ONCE, A BEAUTIFUL QUEEN sat sewing by her window. As she gazed out, she pricked her finger and a drop of blood fell onto the snow-covered ebony frame. "If only I had a daughter with skin as white as snow, lips as red as blood, and hair as black as ebony," she thought. Soon, her wish came true, and she called her baby Snow White. The day after the birth, the Queen died.

A year later, the King took another wife. She, too, was beautiful, but she was also vain. Every day, she asked her magic mirror,

"Mirror, mirror on the wall
Who in the land is fairest of all?"

And it always answered, "You are, O Queen".

As time passed, Snow White grew lovelier and lovelier. One day, when the Queen addressed her mirror, it replied,

"While you are truly fair, O Queen,
Snow White is the fairest to be seen".

Pale with rage, the Queen ordered a huntsman to take the child into the woods and kill her. But he couldn't bear to do such an evil thing, so he left her wandering through the trees.

on the wall . . . Mirror, mirror on the wall . . . Mirror, mirror on the wall . . . Mirror, mirror on the wall . . .

53

Eventually, she stumbled on a cottage owned by seven dwarfs who worked all day in the mines. Snow White was very tired so when the dwarfs came home they found her fast asleep. When she woke, she told them all about the wicked Queen. Moved by her plight, they promised that if she kept house for them, they would look after her. Meanwhile, the Queen faced her mirror.

"Mirror, mirror on the wall
Who in the land is fairest of all?"

And the mirror replied,
"While you are truly fair, O Queen,
Snow White is the fairest to be seen".

When the Queen realized that Snow White was still alive, her anger was terrible. She disguised herself as an old pedlar and set off for the woods. Soon she found the dwarfs' cottage and knocked at the door. The dwarfs had warned Snow White not to let anyone in, but she was a trusting child and the pedlar's wares dazzled her. "Good things, pretty things, very, very cheap," cried the old woman.

When Snow White appeared, the stranger said, "Your bodice is coming undone! Let me tie it with these new laces".

But in a trice, she had pulled them so tight that Snow White fell lifeless to the floor. When the dwarfs returned, they thought she was dead, but once they discovered what had happened and untied her bodice, she began to breathe again.

That night, the Queen questioned her mirror.

"Mirror, mirror on the wall
Who in the land is fairest of all?"

And back came the reply,
*"While you are truly fair, O Queen,
Snow White is the fairest to be seen".*

Instantly the Queen set off for the cottage, changing her disguise and taking with her a stock of combs including a very beautiful one she had dipped in poison.

When she arrived, Snow White refused to open the door but, in the end, the special comb was too tempting. As soon as she got inside, the Queen stuck it in Snow White's hair, and when the poison touched her skin, she fell down senseless. But this time, the dwarfs returned early, and as soon as they removed the poisoned comb, Snow White came back to life.

Later, the Queen turned to her mirror, but it did not give her the message she desperately wanted to hear.
*"While you are truly fair, O Queen,
Snow White is the fairest to be seen."*

Now trembling with hate, she found a big, shiny apple and put poison inside one half. Dressed as an old countrywoman, she knocked at the dwarf's cottage door, but Snow White would only peek out of the window.
"I must not let you in," she said.
"Then take this apple as a present," offered the old woman.
"No," said Snow White, "I cannot".
"Silly girl, don't be afraid. Here, I will cut it in two – half for me, half for you."
Hearing this, Snow White felt safe enough to take a bite, but as soon as she did, she fell down exactly as if she were dead, with no outward sign of what had happened. When the dwarfs found her, they were heartbroken and they placed her in a glass coffin in a clearing near their cottage.

She lay there for many years, until one day a young prince came upon her and instantly lost his heart. He pleaded with the dwarfs to let him take her coffin and they were so moved, they agreed. Then, as the Prince's servants carried her through the woods, they stumbled. The jolt knocked the poisoned apple from her throat and she opened her eyes. The Prince, overjoyed, declared his love for her and asked for her hand in marriage.

Meanwhile, during Snow White's long sleep, the Queen's mirror continued to provide the longed-for answer to her daily question. Then, on the day the young girl awoke, the words her stepmother dreaded most of all came back at her.

"Mirror, mirror on the wall
Who in the land is fairest of all?"
"While you are truly fair, O Queen,
Snow White is the fairest to be seen."

Finally knowing she was beaten, the Queen choked with rage and died, and Snow White lived happily ever after with her Prince.

Familiar story
With surprisingly little variation, this tale is found in the folklore of countries as far apart as Ireland and Turkey, and throughout parts of north and west Africa as well.

56

Anthony McPartlin

"I've always loved Roald Dahl and couldn't get enough of his stories growing up. My mam read them to me at bedtime. This book is funny, compelling, and teaches kids great values."

Setting the Scene

Three nasty farmers, Boggis, Bunce, and Bean, go to battle with Mr Fox. The farmers try to kill him but completely underestimate him and his family – he's not called Fantastic Mr Fox for nothing! Here, the farmers hatch their first murderous plans.

Fantastic Mr Fox
by Roald Dahl
illustrated by Quentin Blake

Mr Fox escapes his enemies . . .

ON A HILL ABOVE THE VALLEY THERE WAS A WOOD. In the wood there was a huge tree.

Under the tree there was a hole.

In the hole lived Mr Fox and Mrs Fox and their four Small Foxes.

Every evening as soon as it got dark, Mr Fox would say to Mrs Fox, "Well, my darling, what shall it be this time? A plump chicken from Boggis? A duck or goose from Bunce? Or a nice turkey from Bean?" And when Mrs Fox had told him what she wanted, Mr Fox would creep down into the valley in the darkness of the night and help himself.

Boggis and Bunce and Bean knew very well what was going on, and it made them wild with rage. They were not men who liked to give anything away. Less still did they like anything to be stolen from them. So every night each of them would take his shotgun and hide in a dark place somewhere on his own farm, hoping to catch the robber.

But Mr Fox was too clever for them. He always approached a farm with the wind blowing in his face, and this meant that if any man were lurking in the shadows ahead, the wind would carry the smell of that man to Mr Fox's nose from far away.

Thus, if Mr Boggis was hiding behind his Chicken House Number One, Mr Fox would smell him out from fifty yards off and quickly change direction, heading for Chicken House Number Four at the other end of the farm.

"Dang and blast that lousy beast!" cried Boggis.

"I'd like to rip his guts out!" said Bunce.

"He must be killed!" cried Bean.

"But how?" said Boggis. "How on earth can we catch the blighter?"

Bean picked his nose delicately with a long finger. "I have a plan," he said.

"You've never had a decent plan yet," said Bunce.

"Shut up and listen," said Bean. "Tomorrow night we will all hide just outside the hole where the fox lives. We will wait there until he comes out. Then... *Bang! Bang-bang-bang.*"

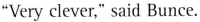

"Very clever," said Bunce. "But first we shall have to find the hole."

"My dear Bunce, I've already found it," said the crafty Bean. "It's up in the wood on the hill. It's under a huge tree..."

58

Declan Donnelly

"When I was young I was given a collection of Roald Dahl books. I read them all but this became my favourite — in fact it is still one of my favourite books of all time."

Setting the Scene

Willy Wonka has put five golden tickets inside chocolate bars. The lucky finders are invited to go on a tour of his amazing chocolate factory and will receive free sweets for life. Four tickets have already been found when the starving Charlie Bucket finds 50p in the snow and uses it to buy some chocolate...

Charlie and the Chocolate Factory

by Roald Dahl illustrated by Quentin Blake

A miraculous find . . .

"I THINK," HE SAID QUIETLY, "I think . . . I'll have just one more of those chocolate bars. The same kind as before, please".

"Why not?" the fat shopkeeper said, reaching behind him again and taking another Whipple-Scrumptious Fudgemallow Delight from the shelf. He laid it on the counter.

Charlie picked it up and tore off the wrapper . . . and *suddenly* . . . from underneath the wrapper. . . there came a brilliant flash of gold.

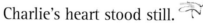

Charlie's heart stood still.

"It's a Golden Ticket!" screamed the shopkeeper, leaping about a foot in the air. "You've got a Golden Ticket! You've found the last Golden Ticket! Hey, would you believe it! Come and look at this, everybody! This kid's found Wonka's last Golden Ticket! There it is! It's right here in his hands!"

It seemed as though the shopkeeper might be going to have a fit. "In my shop, too!" he yelled. "He found it right here in my own little shop! Somebody call the newspapers quick and let them know! Watch out now, sonny! Don't tear it as you unwrap it! That thing's precious!"

In a few seconds, there was a crowd of about twenty people clustering around Charlie, and many more were pushing their way in from the street. Everybody wanted to get a look at the Golden Ticket and at the lucky finder.

stood still . . . Charlie's heart stood still . . . Charlie's heart stood still . . . Charlie's heart stood still . . .

59

"Where is it?" somebody shouted. "Hold it up so all of us can see it!"

"There it is, there!" someone else shouted. "He's holding it in his hands! See the gold shining!"

"How did *he* manage to find it, I'd like to know?" a large boy shouted angrily. "*Twenty* bars a day I've been buying for weeks and weeks!"

"Think of all the free stuff he'll be getting too!" another boy said enviously. "A lifetime supply!"

"He'll need it, the skinny little shrimp!" a girl said, laughing.

Charlie hadn't moved. He hadn't even unwrapped the Golden Ticket from around the chocolate. He was standing very still, holding it tightly with both hands while the crowd pushed and shouted all around him. He felt quite dizzy. There was a peculiar floating sensation coming over him, as though he were floating up in the air like a balloon. His feet didn't seem to be touching the ground at all. He could hear his heart thumping away loudly somewhere in his throat.

... The fat shopkeeper shouted "Leave the kid alone, will you! Make way there! Let him out!" And to Charlie, as he led him to the door, he whispered, "Don't you let *anybody* have it! Take it straight home, quickly, before you lose it! Run all the way and don't stop till you get there, you understand?"

Charlie nodded.

"You know something," the fat shopkeeper said, pausing a moment and smiling at Charlie, "I have a feeling you needed a break like this. I'm awfully glad you got it. Good luck to you, sonny".

"Thank you," Charlie said, and off he went, running through the snow as fast as his legs would go. And as he flew past Mr Willy Wonka's factory, he turned and waved at it and sang out, "I'll be seeing you! I'll be seeing you soon!" And five minutes later he arrived at his own home.

60

June Sarpong

"My great-grandmother could tell the Anansi stories in both English and Ghanaian, and she told them with such enthusiasm that Anansi became my original Spiderman. Whenever I think of him and his tricks, he makes me smile."

Setting the Scene

Anansi the trickster spider is a major figure in the folklore of the Ashanti people in west Africa. Clever and mischievous, Anansi achieves his goals with sheer brainpower rather than size and strength.

Did you know?

★ The traditional Anansi tales were carried to the West Indies by early slaves. In their new home, they were known as "Aunt Nancy" stories.

Anansi the Spider
When Stories Came to Earth
illustrated by Jacqueline Gooden

IN THE TIME OF LONG AGO, there were no stories on Earth for anyone to tell. All the stories that ever were, or ever would be, belonged to Nyame, the sky-god, who kept them locked away beside him in a wooden box.

But Anansi the spider longed to own the stories for himself, so he climbed up to the sky and asked Nyame if they were for sale. "I will sell them," said Nyame. "But I must have three things in payment: Mmoboro the hornets that swarm and sting, Onini the python that swallows men whole, and Osebo the leopard with teeth like spears. But be warned! Many have tried to meet my price, and all have failed."
"I will not fail," replied Anansi, creeping back through the clouds. Now Anansi did not have great size, or strength, or power, or riches, so he had to gain his prize by wits alone.

To deliver Mmoboro, he worked out his first cunning plan. He took a hollow gourd with a hole in it, and a bowl of water, to the hornets' tree. Next, he splashed water all around – on himself and on the hornets too. Finally, he put the bowl on his head like a hat.

"Fools!" he cried out. "Why don't you shelter from the rain?"
"Where should we go?" the hornets asked.
"Here, in this dry gourd," he suggested.
When they had all flown inside, he plugged the hole and delivered the gourd to Nyame.

Next, Anansi cut a long bamboo pole and set off for Onini's house. When he got near, he began to mutter to himself,

"Stupid! Stupid! Stupid!"

"What's wrong Anansi?" enquired the python.

"I am having an argument with my wife. She says you are shorter than this bamboo pole, but I say you are longer."

"We will soon see," said the python, stretching out his body.

"To make sure you don't slip," suggested Anansi, "let me tie your head to the pole".

Once that was done, Anansi bound the rest of the snake to the bamboo with strong vines and carried him up to the sky-god.

Now, only Osebo was left. Anansi went into the forest and dug a deep pit. When he was finished, he covered it with branches and scuttled away. That night, Osebo went prowling and fell straight into the hole. At dawn, Anansi returned. Osebo saw him and cried, "I have fallen into a trap – help me!" So Anansi bent a tall green tree toward the ground and anchored it over the pit. Then he fastened one end of a rope to the tree and dropped the other end down to the leopard. "Here, tie this to your tail," said Anansi. Osebo did as he was told.

"Is it tied tightly?" enquired the spider.

"Yes, very tightly," came the reply.

With that, Anansi cut the bent tree from its anchor so it snapped up, dangling the leopard by his tail. When Osebo was dizzy from dangling, the spider bound his feet and delivered him to Nyame.

"You have paid my full price, Anansi," the sky-god said. "Your clever tricks have won where great warriors and chiefs have lost. From this day on, all stories belong to you." So Anansi brought the box of stories home, and soon they sprung up all over the world in the same way that everywhere you look, spiders' webs mysteriously appear.

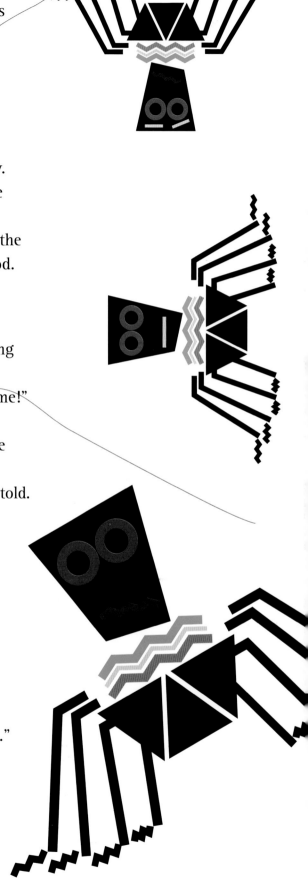

62

Nicki Chapman

"*James and the Giant Peach* is a fantastic children's story. It leads you through a wonderful adventure and lets your imagination run wild!"

Nick Chapman

The world of Roald Dahl

Roald Dahl discovered his talent for writing when he was asked to record his experiences as a World War II fighter pilot for a magazine article. He became a successful adult author, but it was making up bedtime stories for his daughters that started him writing books for children. *James and the Giant Peach* was published in 1961. This poem from the book is recited just before the Giant Peach and its occupants escape from James' nasty aunts Spiker and Sponge. It expresses Dahl's belief that "There is no end to what you can invent".

James and the Giant Peach

by Roald Dahl illustrated by Lane Smith

There Is No Knowing What We Shall See!

"THERE IS NO KNOWING WHAT WE SHALL SEE!"
cried the Centipede.
"We may see a Creature with forty-nine heads
Who lives in the desolate snow,
And whenever he catches a cold (which he dreads)
He has forty-nine noses to blow.

"We may see the venomous Pink-Spotted Scrunch
Who can chew up a man with one bite.
It likes to eat five of them roasted for lunch
And eighteen for its supper at night.

"We may see a Dragon, and
  nobody knows
That we won't see a Unicorn there.
We may see a terrible Monster
  with toes
Growing out of the tufts of
  his hair.

"We may see the sweet little
  Biddy-Bright Hen
So playful, so kind and well-bred;
And such beautiful eggs! You
  just boil them and then
They explode and they
  blow off your head.

Earthworm

Miss Spider

Silkworm

Glow-Worm

Old-Green-Grasshopper

James

Ladybird

Centipede

"A Gnu and a Gnocerous surely you'll see
And that gnormous and gnorrible Gnat
Whose sting when it stings you goes in at the knee
And comes out through the top of your hat.

"We may even get lost and be frozen by frost.
We may die in an earthquake or tremor.
Or nastier still, we may even be tossed
On the horns of a furious Dilemma.

"But who cares! Let us go from this horrible hill!
Let us roll! Let us bowl! Let us plunge!
Let's go rolling and bowling and spinning until
We're away from old Spiker and Sponge!"

64

Terry Waite

"This is a warm and charming tale that reminds us of a time when children could play near railway lines and talk easily to strangers."

Setting the Scene

When their father leaves home suddenly, Roberta, Peter, and Phyllis move with their mother from a big London house to a small cottage in the country. Their new home is beside a railway track, and the children spend hours watching the trains go by.

THIS EXTRACT WAS TAKEN FROM THE LADYBIRD CLASSICS EDITION RETOLD BY JOAN COLLINS.

The Railway Children
by E. Nesbit illustrated by George Buchanan
The old gentleman helps out . . .

THE CHILDREN COULD NOT KEEP AWAY from the railway, and the Station Master said they could visit whenever they liked. Before long they had given the trains names. The 9.15 up was the Green Dragon. The midnight express, which sometimes woke them from their dreams, was the Fearsome Fly by Night.

They made a friend, a fresh-faced old gentleman who travelled on the 9.15. He waved to them as they watched the Green Dragon tear out of its dark lair in the tunnel, and they waved back. They liked to think that perhaps he knew their father in London and would take their love to him.

The porter, whose name was Perks, told them all sorts of fascinating things about trains. You were only allowed to pull the communication cord if you were going to be murdered or something. An old lady had pulled it once because she thought it was the refreshment car bell and ordered a Bath bun when the guard came. Perks also told them about the different kinds of engines. Peter started to collect engine numbers in a notebook.

One day their mother was taken ill, and Peter had to fetch the doctor from the village. He said it was influenza, and gave her some medicine. He also said she should have beef tea, brandy and all sorts of luxuries. The children were very worried.

"We've got to do something!" said Bobbie. "Let's think *hard*."
At last they had an idea. They got a sheet and made a big
notice that read:

LOOK OUT AT THE STATION

They fixed it up on the fence, and pointed at it when the train
went by. Phyllis ran ahead to the station with a letter for the
old gentleman. It told how ill their mother was and what they
needed, and promised to repay him when they grew up. The old
gentleman read it, smiled and put it in his pocket. Then he went
on reading *The Times*.

That evening Perks came to their
door with a big hamper. In it
was everything they had asked
for, and more – peaches, two
chickens, port wine, red roses
and a bottle of Eau-de-Cologne.
There was also a letter from the
old gentleman. He said it was
a pleasure to help, and their
mother was not to be cross
with them for asking.

A fortnight later, another notice
went up:

SHE IS NEARLY
WELL, THANK YOU

Mother *was* very angry at first,
but she knew the children had
only wanted to help.
"You must never, *never* ask
strangers to give us things!" she said earnestly.
"But I must write to thank your old gentleman
for his great kindness."

The world of E. Nesbit

Edith Nesbit was born in
London in 1858. When she
was 21, she married a man
called Hubert Bland and
they had three children.
Like Mother in the story,
Edith had to support her
family when her husband
faced ruin, so she started
writing children's books
and stories. *The Railway
Children*, published in 1906,
was made into an equally
popular film in 1972.

Phillip Schofield

"This book inspired my love of reading. I was five and my class teacher read it to us for 20 minutes each day. I got so engrossed in the adventure, I asked my mum to buy the book (which I still have) so I could race ahead to the end."

Setting the Scene

The Moomin family – Moomintroll, Moominpapa, and Moominmama – live in Moominland, where "unexpected and disturbing things . . . happen". One day, Moomintroll learns about "stars with tails", or comets, and he begins to worry that a big one is headed for Earth. He and his friend Sniff set out for the Observatory, where they can get a closer look.

Comet in Moominland
by Tove Jansson
Which is about having to manage crocodiles . . .

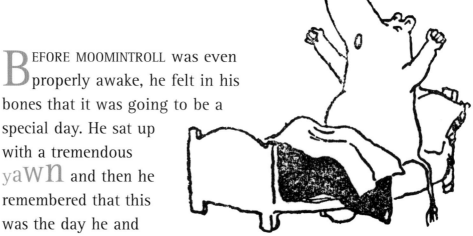

BEFORE MOOMINTROLL was even properly awake, he felt in his bones that it was going to be a special day. He sat up with a tremendous yawn and then he remembered that this was the day he and Sniff were to start their great expedition. He ran to the window to look at the weather. It was still overcast, with the clouds hanging low over the hills, and not a leaf stirred in the garden. Moomintroll was so excited he had almost lost his fear of the comet.

"We'll try to find out where this nasty piece of work is, and then try to stop it coming here," he thought. "But I'd better keep this to myself, because if Sniff got to know he'd be so frightened that he wouldn't be of the smallest use to anybody." Out loud he cried:

"Up you get little animal! We're starting now".

Moominmamma had got up very early to pack their rucksacks, and was bustling to and fro with woolly stockings and packets of sandwiches, while down by the bridge Moominpappa was getting their raft in order.

"Mamma, dear," said Moomintroll, "we can't possibly take all that with us. Everyone will laugh".

"It's cold in Lonely Mountains," said Moominmamma
stuffing in an umbrella and a frying-pan.
"Have you got a compass?"
"Yes," answered Moomintroll, "but couldn't you at least
leave out the plates – we can easily eat off rhubarb leaves".
"As you like, my beloved Moominchild," said his mother,
unearthing the plates from the bottom of the rucksack.
"Now I think everything is ready." And she went down
to the bridge to see them off.

The raft was all ready with hoisted sail, and the silk-monkey
had come down to say goodbye, but she had refused to go
with them because she was afraid of water.

The Muskrat wasn't there because he didn't wish anything
to disturb his contemplation of the uselessness of everything
(and besides, he was rather annoyed with Moomintroll and
Sniff, who had put a hairbrush in his bed).
"Now don't forget to keep on the right side of the river," said
Moominpappa. "I shouldn't mind going along too," he added
rather wistfully, thinking of the adventurous journeys he had
had in his youth with the little wandering Hattifatteners.

Sniff and Moomintroll hugged everyone, the painter was cast
off and the raft began to float down the river.
"Don't forget to give my regards to all the house-troll relatives!"
cried Moominmamma. "The shaggy ones, you know, with round
heads. And put on your woolly trousers when it's cold! The
tummy powder is in the left-hand pocket of the rucksack."

But the raft had already floated round the nearest bend, and
in front of them stretched the Unknown, wild and enticing.

It was late evening. Their rust-red sail hung loosely, and the
river lay silver-grey between its shadowy branches. Not a
bird sang; even the scatter-brained chaffinches, which
usually twitter from morning till night, were silent.

The world of Tove Jansson

Born in 1914, Finnish writer
and illustrator Tove Jansson
was the child of artistic
parents: her father was a
sculptor, and her mother
was an illustrator who
designed 165 Finnish
stamps. Jansson studied
painting in Finland,
Sweden, and France,
but she mainly lived and
worked alone on a small
island in the Gulf of
Finland. She died in
2001 at the age of 86.

Did you know?

★ In total, Tove Jansson
produced nine Moomin
stories. Although her
family were Finnish, they
were part of a Swedish-
speaking minority, and
she wrote all her books
in Swedish.

★ Today, the Moomin
books have been
translated into 34
languages including
Korean, Persian, Faroese,
Saami (spoken in
Lapland), and Lettish
(spoken in Latvia).

68

"Not one adventure in a whole day," said Sniff, who was taking his turn at steering now the current was slower. "Just grey banks and grey banks and grey banks, and not even an adventure."
"I think it's very adventurous to float down a winding river," said Moomintroll. "You never know what you'll meet round the next corner. You always want adventures, Sniff, and when they come you're so frightened you don't know what to do."
"Well, I'm not a lion," said Sniff reproachfully. "I like small adventures. Just the right size."

At that moment the raft floated slowly round a bend. "Here's just the right sized adventure for you," said Moomintroll pointing. Right in front of them lay what looked like a heap of big grey logs on a sandbank – and the logs were arranged in the secret pattern – a star with a tail!

"There it is again!" screamed Sniff. Suddenly the logs began to move, and produced legs, and then the whole mass slid silently under the water.

"Crocodiles!" exclaimed Moomintroll, jumping to the rudder. "Let's hope they don't chase us!"

The river seemed to be swarming with the monsters whose eyes shone pale green on its surface, and yet more of the fearful grey shadowy bodies were slithering down the muddy bank into the water.

Sniff sat in the stern, stiff with fear, and only moved when a crocodile lifted its nose beside him, when he beat it wildly over the head with an oar. It was a terrible moment.

Tails thrashed the water; giant mouths, bristling with needle-sharp teeth, snapped angrily, and the raft rocked up and down in the most alarming way.

Moomintroll and Sniff clung tightly to the mast and
screamed for help, while the raft, caught by a little wind
that had fortunately just got up, began to make headway down
the river. The crocodiles followed in a long line, their cruel jaws
a-gape.

Sniff hid his face in his paws, while Moomintroll, who was so
frightened he hardly knew what he was doing, got the woolly
trousers out of the rucksack and threw them to their pursuers.

This distracted the crocodiles' attention at once. They tore at
the woolly trousers and fought so furiously over them
that by the time every bit was devoured Sniff and Moomintroll
were miles away.

"Well, strike me pink!" exclaimed Moomintroll.
"Are you satisfied with that adventure?"

"You screamed too," said Sniff. "Did I?" said Moomintroll.
"I don't remember. Anyway it was a good thing mamma
put in those woolly trousers."

Darkness was closing in over the river, so after landing the
raft they built a fire between the roots of a big tree, and fried

pancakes for supper,
which they ate, in
their fingers, one
by one as they came
out of the frying pan.
Then they crept into
their sleeping-bags
and the night fell.

70

Fern Britton

"I found this story in a fairytale book I won when I was at school. The pictures in that version showed a crown on the frog's head, and I thought it was funny how the princess didn't realize he was special. My girls love this story too."

Fern

The world of the brothers Grimm

Jacob and Wilhelm Grimm were born in Germany in 1785 and 1786 respectively. Recording traditional folk stories was their life's work, and they published their first book in 1812. *The Frog Prince*, which dates from the Middle Ages, was also called *The Well of the World's End*.

The Frog Prince
by Jacob and Wilhelm Grimm
illustrated by Julie Downing

ONE SUMMER EVENING, a young Princess was cooling herself beside an old well. To pass the time, she tossed a beautiful golden ball into the air. But suddenly, in one careless moment, she threw it so high that it curved over the water and fell in.

The Princess peered after it, but the well was so deep she couldn't see the bottom. When she realized her ball was lost, she began to weep. Suddenly, a gentle voice broke the silence: "Princess, why are you weeping?"

When she looked up, the Princess saw that a frog had stuck its head out of the water.
"My ball has fallen into the well," she told him.
"Don't worry, Princess, I will bring it back. But if I do, you must promise to let me live with you and be your friend."
Quickly, she replied, "Oh yes! Anything you ask".
But really she thought, "What nonsense! Frogs sit on the water with other frogs – this one cannot come home with me".

Immediately, the frog dived in and returned with the precious plaything. But as soon as he dropped it at the Princess's feet, she picked it up and ran off home.
"Wait, wait!" called the frog. "You promised to take me with you." But she didn't look back.

The next day, as the Princess sat down to dinner, she heard strange tapping on the stairs, then knocking at the door. From the other side of the door, a voice spoke:

"Open the door, my princess dear,
Open the door to thy true love here!
And mind the words that thou and I said
By the fountain cool in the greenwood shade".

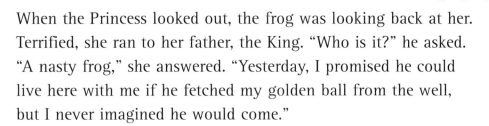

When the Princess looked out, the frog was looking back at her. Terrified, she ran to her father, the King. "Who is it?" he asked. "A nasty frog," she answered. "Yesterday, I promised he could live here with me if he fetched my golden ball from the well, but I never imagined he would come."

"You made a promise, so you must keep it," ordered the King. "Let him in." And she did as she was told.
"Lift me up so I can sit next to you," asked the frog.
She did this and he said, "Put your plate next to me so I can eat from it".
She did this too, and after he had finished eating, he made one last request. "I am very tired. Carry me upstairs and tuck me into your bed." So the Princess placed him carefully on her pillow and he fell asleep beside her.

In the morning when she woke, the Princess looked for the ugly green frog, but he was gone. And in his place, standing by her bed, was a very tall, very handsome prince.
"A wicked fairy turned me into a frog," he told her. "But you kept your promise faithfully, and that has broken her spell."
And the Prince swept her away to his father's kingdom, married her in great splendour, and loved her as long as he lived.

72

Eamonn Holmes

"*Aladdin* always transported me from mundane reality to a world of heroes and villains. But most of all, the adventure made me aware of the difference between power (in the form of the lamp) in the hands of good and power in the hands of evil."

Setting the Scene

The story of Aladdin and his enchanted lamp is one of the ancient and well-loved *Tales from the Arabian Nights*. The story begins with the appearance of a wicked sorcerer who pretends to be the boy's uncle. He knows that only one person can open the cave that holds unimaginable riches, including a mysterious lamp. That person is the boy, Aladdin.

Aladdin
and the Enchanted Lamp
illustrated by Nilesh Mistry

Aladdin explores a fantastic cave . . .

WHEN ALADDIN AND THE SORCERER had passed through the teeming bazaar and into the hills beyond, the boy grew tired, but the old man urged him on. At last, they came to a deep valley.

"Stop!" said the sorcerer. "Gather some sticks and make a fire." Soon a bright blaze leapt into the air. The sorcerer threw a handful of incense into the flames and whispered strange words. Suddenly, the earth trembled and split to reveal a marble slab pierced with a copper ring.

"My child, you must lift this stone," cried the sorcerer. "Then, if you do as I tell you, we will both be richer than all the sultans in the world." Aladdin took hold of the ring and the stone moved away.

"Go down the steps and you will see four halls piled with gold and silver. Pass through, but do not touch. Beyond the fourth hall, you will find a wondrous garden with trees that bear exquisite fruit, but do not go near them. On the far side, set on a pedestal, you will discover a lamp; take this and bring it to me. Once it is safely in your hands, you may pick the fruit."

Aladdin crept into the cave and found just what the sorcerer had described. The gold and silver treasure dazzled him, but when he reached the garden, he was enchanted by what he saw: on every branch were shining, multi-coloured fruits. Remembering his uncle's words, he found the lamp and tucked it into his robe.

Then he began to gather fruits for himself, but he didn't know that they were really pearls, rubies, topazes, sapphires, and emeralds bigger and more brilliant than anyone had ever seen. His eyes shone, and he stuffed jewels inside his clothing until he could hardly move.

Spirit slave

Aladdin does manage to get out of the cave with the help of a powerful genie. In Arabic folklore, genies are supernatural spirits that appear in human and animal form. Sometimes the word is spelt *djin*, *jinn*, or *jinnee*.

"I am the slave of the lamp."

When he got back to the sorcerer, he could not get up the stairs. "Uncle," he shouted, "give me your hand".

"First give me the lamp," came the reply. But the stairs were so narrow, and the boy's clothing so full of jewels, that Aladdin couldn't pull the lamp out. The sorcerer, flying into a blind rage, threw more incense into the fire and uttered his magic words. Instantly, the massive stone closed over the earth, leaving Aladdin sealed in the velvety darkness.

Laurence Llewelyn-Bowen

"The description and detail have an old-fashioned and very evocative feel to them — my children love all the Narnia stories and they seem to get better as they go on."

Setting the scene

During the Second World War, Peter, Edmund, Susan, and Lucy are evacuated to the countryside. During their stay, they discover an old wardrobe that leads to the enchanted land of Narnia. At first, only Lucy finds her way there, and the others tease her mercilessly when she tries to tell them about her adventure. Later, during a game of hide-and-seek, Edmund discovers Narnia for himself.

The Lion, the Witch and the Wardrobe
by C.S. Lewis illustrated by Pauline Baynes
Edmund follows Lucy to her magical place . . .

EDMUND CAME INTO THE ROOM just in time to see Lucy vanishing into the wardrobe. He at once decided to get into it himself – not because he thought it was a particularly good place to hide but because he wanted to go on teasing her about her imaginary country. He opened the door. There were the coats hanging up as usual, and a smell of mothballs, and darkness

and silence, and no sign of Lucy. "She thinks I'm Susan come to catch her," said Edmund to himself, "and so she's keeping very quiet at the back". He jumped in and shut the door, forgetting what a very foolish thing this is to do. Then he began feeling about for Lucy in the dark. He had expected to find her in a few seconds and was very surprised when he did not. He decided to open the door again and let in some light. But he could not find the door either. He didn't like this at all and began groping wildly in every direction; he even shouted out, "Lucy! Lu! Where are you? I know you're here".

There was no answer and Edmund noticed that his own voice had a curious sound – not the sound you expect in a cupboard, but a kind of open-air sound. He also noticed that he was unexpectedly cold; and then he saw a light.

"Thank goodness," said Edmund, "the door must have swung open of its own accord". He forgot all about Lucy and went towards the light, which he thought was the open door of the wardrobe. But instead of finding himself stepping out into the spare room he found himself stepping out from the shadow of some thick dark fir trees into an open place in the middle of a wood.

There was crisp, dry snow under his feet and more snow lying on the branches of the trees. Overhead there was pale blue sky, the sort of sky one sees on a fine winter day in the morning. Straight ahead of him he saw between the tree trunks the sun, just rising, very red and clear. Everything was perfectly still, as if he were the only living creature in that country. There was not even a robin or a squirrel among the trees, and the wood stretched as far as he could see in every direction. He shivered.

He now remembered that he had been looking for Lucy: and also how unpleasant he had been to her about the "imaginary country" which now turned out not to have been imaginary at all. He thought that she must be somewhere quite close and so he shouted, "Lucy! Lucy! I'm here too – Edmund".

There was no answer.

The world of C. S. Lewis

Born in Belfast in 1898, Clive Staples Lewis was a professor at Cambridge University and the author of several books about Christianity. *The Lion, the Witch and the Wardrobe*, published in 1950, was the first of his *Chronicles of Narnia*, which were written for children. Six further *Chronicles* followed, with the final title, *The Last Battle*, appearing in 1956.

Did you know?

★ The immediate inspiration for *The Lion, the Witch and the Wardrobe* was a series of nightmares Lewis had about lions.

★ Lewis was a close friend of J.R.R. Tolkien's. Many experts believe that Tolkien would never have completed *The Lord of the Rings* without Lewis's help and encouragement.

★ Although Lewis wanted his Narnia books to be entertaining in their own right, he also intended them as a retelling of the Christian story in fairytale form.

76

Tony Blair

Treasure Island
by Robert Louis Stevenson
illustrated by David Frankland

Hunting for treasure . . .

Setting the scene

Young Jim Hawkins' adventure begins when he finds a mysterious map that shows where an infamous pirate, Captain Flint, buried his treasure. Soon, Jim and his friends Dr Livesey and Squire Trelawny set sail for a far-away island with a crew that includes the one-legged cook Long John Silver.

This extract was taken from the Ladybird Classics edition retold by Joyce Faraday.

WITH PICKS AND SHOVELS, we set out to find Captain Flint's treasure. The men were armed to the teeth. Silver had two guns and a cutlass. As I was a prisoner, I had a rope tied round my waist. Silver held the other end. In spite of his promise to keep me safe, I did not trust him.

As we went, the men talked about the chart. On the back of it was written: 'TALL TREE, SPY-GLASS SHOULDER, BEARING A POINT
TO THE N. OF N.N.E.
SKELETON ISLAND E.S.E. AND BY E.
TEN FEET'.

So we were looking for a tall tree on a hill. The men were in high spirits, and Silver and I could not keep up with them.

Suddenly there was a shout from one of the men in front. The others ran towards him, full of hope. But it was not treasure he had found. At the foot of the tree lay a human skeleton.

The men looked down in horror. The few rags of clothing that hung on the bones showed that the man had been a sailor. The skeleton was stretched out straight, the feet pointing one way and the arms, raised above the head, pointing in the opposite direction.

Yo-ho-ho and a bottle of rum . . . Yo-ho-ho and a bottle of rum . . . Yo-ho-ho and a bottle of rum . . .

77

"This here's one of Flint's little jokes!" cried Silver. "These bones point E.S.E. and E. This is one of the men he killed, and he's laid him here to point the way!"

The men felt a chill in their hearts, for they had all lived in fear of Flint. "But he's dead," said one of them.

"Aye, sure enough, he's dead and gone below," said another pirate. "But if ever a ghost walked, it would be Flint's." "Aye," said a third man. "I tell you, I don't like to hear 'Fifteen Men' sung now, for it was the only song he ever sang."

Silver put an end to their talk and we moved on, but I noticed that now the men spoke softly and kept together. Just the thought of Flint was enough to fill them with terror.

At the top of the hill we rested. In whispers, the men still talked of Flint. "Ah, well," said Silver, "you praise your stars he's dead." Suddenly, from the trees ahead, a thin, trembling voice struck up the well-known song:

"Fifteen men on the Dead Man's Chest – Yo-ho-ho and a bottle of rum!"

I have never seen men so dreadfully affected as these pirates. The men were rooted to the spot. The colour drained from their faces as they stared ahead in terror. Even Silver was shaking, but he was the first to pull himself together.

"I'm here to get that treasure!" he roared. "I was never feared of Flint in life, and by the Powers, I'll face him dead!"

Long John Silver gave them all fresh heart, and they picked up their tools and set off again.

The world of Robert Louis Stevenson
Born in Edinburgh in 1850, Robert Louis Stevenson was a sickly child who couldn't read until he was seven. Despite his lifelong poor health (now thought to have been caused by tuberculosis), he travelled all around the world and became famous for his adventure stories. Stevenson and his family ended up living in Samoa, where he died very suddenly just before his 44th birthday.

Did you know?

★ *Treasure Island* was first published in 1881, as a serial in *Young Folks* magazine. The first edition of the book, which came out in 1883, had no illustrations except a drawing of the map.

★ Stevenson based the character of Long John Silver on his friend, the writer W. E. Henley, who had lost one foot.

★ The "Dead Man's Chest" mentioned in the song refers to a Caribbean island of that name Stevenson discovered during his research.

Yo-ho-ho and a bottle of rum . . . Yo-ho-ho and a bottle of rum . . . Yo-ho-ho and a bottle of rum . . .

78

A tale is born

Treasure Island came to life during the summer of 1881, when Stevenson was staying with his family in Scotland. To amuse the children, he and his stepson drew a treasure map, and Stevenson began to write a story to go with it. Every evening, he would read out what he had written that day. Joining in the spirit, his father contributed a list of what Billy Bones might have kept in his sea-chest, and his son included this detail in the published version.

We soon saw ahead a huge tree that stood high above the others. The thought of what lay near that tree made the men's fears fade, and they moved faster. Silver hobbled on his crutch. I could tell from the evil in his eyes that, if he got his hands on the gold, he would cut all our throats and sail away.

The men now broke into a run, but not for long. They had come to the edge of a pit. At the bottom lay bits of wood and the broken handle of a pickaxe. It was clear for all to see that the treasure had gone!

The pirates jumped down into the hole and began to dig with their hands. Silver knew that they would turn on him at any moment.

"We're in a tight spot, Jim," he whispered. The look of hate in his eyes had gone. With the pirates against him, he needed me again. Once more he had changed sides.

The pirates scrambled out of the pit and stood facing Silver and me. The leader raised his arm to charge, but before a blow was struck, three musket shots rang out and two pirates fell. The three men left ran for their lives. From out of the wood ran the doctor and Ben Gunn, who had saved us in the nick of time.

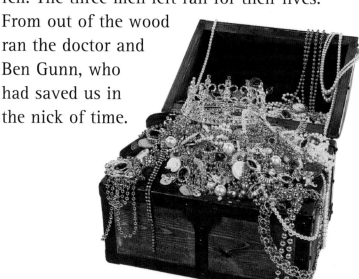

Pirates did steal gold and jewels, but more often their "treasure" was bales of silk or cotton, barrels of rum, tobacco, or weapons.

I'm as clever as clever . . . I'm as clever as clever . . . I'm as clever as clever . . . I'm as clever as clever . . .

79

Joan MacKichan

"I have always found A. A. Milne's world to be a magical place. I love his poems and I enjoy reading them as much now as I did when I was a child."

Joan x

The End
by A. A. Milne
illustrated by E. H. Shepard

When I was One,
I had just begun.

When I was Two
I was nearly new.

When I was Three
I was hardly Me.

When I was Four
I was not much more.

When I was Five
I was just alive.

But now I am Six, I'm as clever as clever.
So I think I'll be six now for ever and ever.

Acknowledgements

Dorling Kindersley gratefully acknowledges the following, for permission to reproduce copyright material in this anthology:

Thomas and the Guard: first published 1990 by William Heinemann Ltd. Used here with permission from Egmont Books Ltd, London. *Thomas and Friends* © Gullane (Thomas) Ltd 2003;
Why Do Kittens Purr?: text © 2003 Marion D. Bauer, illustrations © 2003 Henry Cole. Extract reproduced by permission of Simon & Schuster Books for Young Readers, an imprint of Simon & Schuster Children's Publishing Division;
Paddington Bear: text copyright © 1999 Michael Bond. Used by permission of HarperCollins Publishers Ltd. Illustrations copyright © R.W. (Bob) Alley;
Where the Wild Things Are: extract from WHERE THE WILD THINGS ARE by Maurice Sendak published by Bodley Head. Used by permission of The Random House Group Ltd;
The Lion Who Wanted to Love: taken from THE LION WHO WANTED TO LOVE by Giles Andreae and David Wojtowycz. First published in 1997 by Orchard Books, a division of the Watts Publishing Group Ltd, London, England.
The Three Little Pigs: illustrations from THE PUFFIN BABY AND TODDLER TREASURY (Puffin 1998). Copyright © Paul Howard. Reproduced by permission;
Hairy Maclary from Donaldson's Dairy: text and illustrations reproduced by permission © Lynley Dodd. Published in Puffin Books;
Winter Story: text © 1980 Jill Barklem. Illustrations © 1980 Jill Barklem. Used by permission of HarperCollins Publishers Ltd;
Clarice Bean That's Me: taken from CLARICE BEAN THAT'S ME by Lauren Child. First published in 1999 by Orchard Books, a division of the Watts Publishing Group Ltd., London, England.
The Tale of Peter Rabbit: text and illustrations from *The Tale of Peter Rabbit* by Beatrix Potter, copyright © Frederick Warne & Co., 1902, 2002;
Flower Fairies: *The Song of the Geranium Fairy* and *The Song of the Red Clover Fairy* illustrations and poems by Cicely Mary Barker, copyright © The Estate of Cicely Mary Barker, 1944, 1948, 1990, reproduced by permission of Frederick Warne & Co.;
The Gingerbread Man: illustrations from THE PUFFIN BABY AND TODDLER TREASURY (Puffin 1998). Copyright © Peter Bowman. Reproduced by permission;
Can't You Sleep, Little Bear?: extract and illustration from CAN'T YOU SLEEP, LITTLE BEAR? written by Martin Waddell and illustrated by Barbara Firth. Text © 1988 Martin Waddell, illustrations © 1988 Barbara Firth. Reproduced by permission of Walker Books Ltd, London SE11 5HJ;
Little Red: text © Sarah, Duchess of York, illustrations by Sam Williams © 2003 David Bennett. Abridged extract reproduced by permission of Simon & Schuster Books for Young Readers, an imprint of Simon & Schuster Children's Publishing Division;

The Cuckoo's Trick: from *Atticus the Storyteller's 100 Greek Myths* by Lucy Coats, illustrated by Anthony Lewis. Published by Orion Children's Books;
The Emperor's New Clothes: taken from HANS ANDERSEN'S FAIRY TALES chosen by Naomi Lewis and illustrated by Philip Gough. Collection copyright © Naomi Lewis, 1981. Illustrations copyright © Philip Gough, 1981. Reproduced by permission of Penguin Books Ltd;
The Very Noisy Night: text © 1999 Diana Hendry. Illustrations © 1999 Jane Chapman. Used by permission of Little Tiger Press;
Hansel and Gretel: illustrations by Claire Pound from *Hansel and Gretel (Ladybird Read it Yourself)*, copyright © Ladybird Books Ltd, 1998;
Alfie's New School: text © 2004 Jenny Eclair;
Greyfriars Bobby: from GREYFRIARS BOBBY copyright 1995 by Ruth Brown, first published by Andersen Press Ltd., London, also published by Red Fox;
Peter Pan: abridged extract taken from *Peter Pan* by J. M. Barrie used by permission of Great Ormond Street Hospital Children's Charity;
Snow White: illustrations copyright © 2002 Belinda Downes;
Fantastic Mr Fox: text copyright © Roald Dahl Nominee Ltd, 1970. Illustrations © Quentin Blake, 1996. First published by George Allen and Unwin, 1970. Published in Puffin Books, 1974. Reissued with new illustrations 1996;
Charlie and the Chocolate Factory: text copyright © Roald Dahl Nominee Ltd. 1964. Illustrations © Quentin Blake, 1995. Published in Great Britain by George Allen & Unwin, 1967. Published by Puffin Books 1973. Reissued with new illustrations, 1995;
James and the Giant Peach: text copyright © Roald Dahl Nominee Ltd, 1961. Illustration © Lane Smith, from *The Roald Dahl Treasury*, first published by Jonathan Cape Ltd, 1997. Published in Puffin Books 2003;
The Railway Children: extract and illustrations from *The Railway Children (Ladybird Classics)* by E. Nesbit, retold by Joan Collins and illustrated by George Buchanan, copyright © Ladybird Books Ltd, 1994;
Comet in Moominland: text and illustrations © estate of Tove Jansson. Extract reproduced by permission. Published in Puffin Books;
The Lion, the Witch and the Wardrobe: by C.S. Lewis copyright © C.S. Lewis Pte. Ltd, 1950. Extract reprinted by permission. Illustrations by Pauline Baynes copyright © C.S. Lewis Pte. Ltd;
Treasure Island: extract and illustrations from *Treasure Island (Ladybird Classics)* by Robert Louis Stevenson, retold by Joyce Faraday and illustrated by David Frankland, copyright © Ladybird Books Ltd, 1994;
The End: text from *Now We Are Six* © A.A. Milne. Copyright under the Berne Convention. Published by Egmont Books Limited, London and used with permission. Recorded by permission of the Trustees of the Pooh Properties. Illustration: copyright E.H. Shepard and Egmont Books Ltd. Reproduced by permission of Curtis Brown, London.

Every effort has been made to trace the copyright holders. Dorling Kindersley would like to hear from any copyright holder not acknowledged.

Dorling Kindersley would like to thank the following for their kind permission to reproduce their photographs:

Photographs of the stars on the jacket and inside the book: ITV for pictures of Ant & Dec; Joe Miles/ITV for picture of Phillip Schofield; Tara Sgroi for the picture of Sarah, The Duchess of York; picture of Fearne Cotton copyright BBC; Grant Squibb for the picture of June Sarpong; Corbis: Steve Sands/New York Newswire for the picture of Kate Winslet; Katz: Eleanor Bentall for the picture of Stephen Fry; Pa Photos: Harveya Anthony Harvey for the picture of Jerry Hall; Retna Pictures Ltd: Christopher Barker for the picture of Pete Waterman; Rex Features: Ray Tang for the picture of Sarah Brown, Woman's Own for the picture of Richard E. Grant. All the celebrities, press offices, and agents who provided photographs.

Key: a-above; c-centre; b-below; l-left; r-right; t-top

DK Images: © Judith Miller/Dorling Kindersley/Lyon & Turnbull Ltd 74-75b (wardrobe); © Paddington & Co Ltd., 2004 12bl; London Dungeon 74-75b (hat); National Railway Museum, York 64-65b (train), 64-65b (whistle). Great Ormond Street Hospital: 51cr.

All other images: © Dorling Kindersley. For further information, see www.dkimages.com

Dorling Kindersley would also like to thank:

All the publishers, writers, and illustrators who have kindly let us use their material free of charge. Sarah-Jane Barrett, Emily Ford, and Nicola Withers in Puffin for their help and advice; Jacqueline Gooden for original digital artworks; Kate Ledwith, Sarah Mills, and Hayley Smith for DK Picture Library research.

Victoria Chilcott would like to thank:

All the stars for their time and considerable effort and their agents/managers, particularly James Grant Management. A big thank you to Al Petrie for reading so beautifully on the CD and Mark Ralph for his hard work and musical brilliance producing the stories and Ian Pearce for his sound effects. Chelsea Chandler and Nick Cox at the Farm Post Production Company for giving their time and equipment for free and for all the support and help I received from the television producers who opened their little black books. A thank you to Phillippa Barton for being so organised, capable, and calm, but my biggest thank you goes to Nelly Duffy for all her hard work, enthusiasm, and commitment to the book.